Enthralled

By J.T. McGee

Valenza Publishing

Valenza Publishing
Hadley, NY 12835

First published in 2025

ISBN:
Paperback - 979-8-9919345-1-0

Praise for J.T. and Thrall

More from Valenza Publishing

J.T. McGee

Thrall

Ella M. Hayes

Bookends

Jamie Norton

The Second Act Comeback

Andrew Valenza

Empire of the Void
Lost World of the Void

Three Short Horror Stories

Dedication

Incredibly grateful to my family, friends, and students for their support.

SLEEPLESS

Gavin couldn't remember the last time he slept through the night. He stared at the ceiling of the cabin's lone bedroom. Gavin questioned whether or not staying at his Uncle's place would be best. Months had passed since he had tried to destroy the Gläm forces amassing in the Berkshires. The deciding factor for him was that it was the best location to minimize collateral damage. If they came to hurt him here, they would find him alone. The same couldn't be said for his Grandmother's place.

The leaves had mostly fallen and it had started to get cold out. There was plenty of firewood to be had between his efforts and his Uncle John's. Yet no fire smoldered in the wood stove despite the chill. Even so, he was covered in sweat, his mind raced in circles around the unknown. There were still so many things left unanswered for him since becoming tangled up in the sinister affairs of the Gläm. His brother Nathan's whereabouts and condition were a mystery. Whether or not they had been successful in taking out the Gläm was also uncertain. He hadn't heard from Madson or Becker, which was probably a good thing. After all, sometimes no news is good news.

When they parted ways, they had agreed that contact was to be minimal. Becker had even insisted on a code word, *phantasmagoria*, to be safe. Or, perhaps just to show off his vocabulary.

Gavin desperately wanted to see Linda and Clara but he knew any contact with them would be dangerous. He hated the way things had gone with Linda. In his mind, he could hardly remember a time when he didn't love her. His daughter, Clara, was the best thing that ever happened to him. The day she was born was one of the most amazing things he had ever been a part of. Even though he knew that not seeing them was the best thing he could do to keep them out of harm's way, it still tore him up inside when he was alone with his thoughts.

A coyote yipped from the tree line. Gavin was up and on his feet in an instant. The sawed-off shotgun from his bedside table was in his hand before his feet hit the floor. His head cleared quickly and he realized what it was. He had tried to secure the cabin as best he could, setting up small alarms and tripwires so that any unannounced company would be revealed to him.

At times, he missed the convenience of more modern living but, given his situation, there were some benefits to being in the middle of the woods. At night it was dark, very dark, and if one didn't know their way around, there was a catastrophically strong chance that someone was going to trip or bump into something. The notion of having a natural defense of sorts, provided a small sense of security.

Gavin found that at times he bordered on paranoia, but usually thought it best to err on the side of caution. He had seen first hand his enemy's capabilities. His Uncle John had perished right before Gavin's eyes as a result of underestimating the Gläm. When they took action it was sudden and devastating.

Gavin had found a box of Christmas ornaments in the back of John's closet. In it were strings of tiny bells no doubt meant for trimming a tree during the holidays. So, just like one of those corny kids' movies, he used fishing lines to construct tiny tripwires around doorways. In a matter of weeks, he had become accustomed to them, but there were a few mishaps after he had first installed them. Which, if anyone had been around, it would have been very funny to witness. He was content to chuckle to himself amid the commotion. His grandmother had always said that being able to laugh at yourself was important and in moments like those he couldn't help but think of her.

Gavin got himself situated back in bed hoping that sleep would soon come. He glanced over at the gun to ensure it was still there. It provided some comfort knowing it was at the ready. If it had been the tinkling of bells instead of yelps, he would have needed it. Laying there in bed, he would imagine how they would come for him; smashing through a window, kicking down the door and bursting into the room or overtaking him with sheer numbers and pinning him to his mattress. Gavin would envision their attacks and rehearse his retaliations in his head, most nights until the sun rose.

Tonight, his thoughts wandered into memory, remembering his Grandmother. They had gone to a zoo once when he was younger, where there was an exhibit that housed a Grizzly bear. It was a man-made reconstruction of a rock cave with a little waterfall and a honeysuckle bush nestled at its peak, all wrapped around by a cast iron fence. The bear was huge, even at a distance. Gavin remembered its eyes. They seemed lost and complacent. Every rock tossed, finger pointed, each poke and prod took its toll. The massive creature looked defeated and sat there staring back at him. Gavin remembered starting to cry and squeezing his grandmother's hand. She had been unaware that he was upset. She looked down at him and asked what was wrong, but he could not articulate a response. Nor could he look away from the bear. There was a longing that weighed on him but he still could not break its gaze. His grandmother had asked a second time but he did not hear her. Worried for him, she scooped Gavin up and headed toward the next exhibit. His eyes were still locked on the beast even as it became a shadow and eventually passed from his sight. Gavin heard it bellow as he left. He had never heard a bear roar before but somehow instinctively he knew that this wasn't one. He felt himself tossing and turning. In his dream, he was being pulled to look away from his grandmother. His gaze slowly drifted down to his hand, it was being held by someone. His vision followed up the wrist to the arm and there was Nathan. His older brother wasn't usually in this dream. Nathan wore a puzzled look as he stared back at Gavin. For some unknowable reason his gaze was unbearable.

No, Gavin knew fully well the reason he couldn't look his brother in the eye.

He writhed and twisted in his bed, drenched in sweat,

restrained by the sheets and covers that were now curling about his limbs like tendrils.

"*You tried to kill me.*" Gavin heard, unmistakably, the voice of Nathan from their childhood.

Gavin shot up to a sitting position, sweaty and breathing hard.

He rubbed his hands across his stubbled cheeks, fixed his covers and pulled them up over his head like when he was a kid, trapped within an illusion of safety.

As he struggled to drift back to sleep a small grin stretched across his face because he knew now the plight of the bear.

SCARS

Nathan traced the scar on his hand as Xavier loomed over him. He was seated and slouched, staring down at the insignia burned into his palm from the explosion intended to kill him and the Immortals. Nathan ran his index finger along the ridges of the thick scar tissue, mindlessly following the curves of the pattern with his fingertip. Lost in thought, the sensation was a soothing form of distraction. Lately, he had started questioning a lot of things. Whether or not he had been used to achieve the aims of others was an ever present and nagging enigma to him. His own brother had tried to stop him, to the extent of blowing up the estate in the Berkshires. When your own flesh and blood was willing to take such drastic measures, make such terrible sacrifices, and with such extreme resolve, it was cause for evaluation.

Xavier was talking shop, acquisitions, and business plans for expansion into new territory, rattling on about real estate and properties. He had healed as if the explosion had never happened. "*You're not paying attention*," a duo of voices scolded Nathan in his head.

The correction was enough to snap him out of his daze. He straightened himself up in his chair and found Xavier's icy blue stare intent upon him. His long bony hands were planted on the teak-wood desk. His face, mere inches from Nathan's.

I wonder how long he's been there like that, Nathan thought to himself.

"Longer than you realize and longer than I would like," Xavier impatiently replied aloud. "What has got you so distracted today?" he asked almost compassionately, yet a tinge of irritation could be heard in his tone. He eased himself back into a chair across from Nathan. The man always appeared to be almost floating in his movements as if he were sliding or gliding. Gravity seemed to be less taxing on Immortals compared to humans.

"Will I stay like this?"

"Like what?" Xavier snapped.

"Burnt."

Nathan's reply was sharper than Xavier would've tolerated from anyone else. The wounded expression on his face combined with the rippled flesh from the fire caused Xavier to take pause. He sighed in an effort to release some of the intensity from the conversation. As of late, he'd become frustrated with Nathan's apparent ennui. Xavier paused, rubbing his chin while he contemplated, the fact that he was relying on Nathan to help expand the Gläm control over a new territory. The pressure must be getting to Nathan. He pondered the situation before lashing out verbally. If Nathan failed, it would not bode well for any of their kind. It would also be a reflection on Xavier and he hated looking the fool. Despite Xavier's own building frustrations and concerns, he decided it may be best to opt for tolerance and patience towards Nathan.

"Perhaps," he mused, trying to find the right words, "you may remain as you are, but perhaps, you may not. What difference does it really make? It is not as though our kind would care." Xavier swept his hand in a cavalier fashion parallel to the desk.

"I've just been thinking that having to look like this for an eternity was not part of the deal."

"The deal…" Xavier rose from his seat, his fury mounting on his countenance, his patience had worn thin. He was only inches from Nathan's face again. His words boomed throughout the office, as well as, inside Nathan's head. "The *deal* was that you would be granted immortality. The *deal* was that you would be like a lord over a whole new land. The *deal* was that you were to continue where your father left off. It is foolish to be concerned with appearances. Power and control are what we are after." Xavier pounded his fist on the desk for emphasis, cracking it deeply and leaving a jagged crater. "*Am I making myself clear?*" His question was a growl rumbling behind Nathan's eyes.

Nathan looked up at him returning his stare. "Crystal."

Nathan's mind flashed to the day the explosion erupted and tore through the ceremony. The Immortals in attendance, there to celebrate him entering the last stage of development, survived the blast. The attack would have killed him if it were not for Xavier's intervention. He wondered if he would have been better off if his brother's plan had been successful in the Berkshires. His face and arm were horribly burned, the event meant to mark his acceptance ruined and his fiancee, Alice, torn to shreds by a shower of glass.

Loss. Sacrifice. Disfigurement.

"For what?"

A voice within him spoke.

His ward responded. *"This too shall pass."*

ANTIQUUS LIBELLUS
SERVATOR GAVIN CROSS

By far one of the most disgusting aspects of the Gläm are the twisted bonds they create with their livestock. Peelers (as they are often referred to) are even marked as cattle with tattoos or brands. The Gläm have far surpassed being simple parasites. Their origins may be from the deep sea but it would seem that they've learned a lot on land. When they feed, the Gläm secrete a substance like heroin or morphine. This not only allows them to feed but also creates an addicted victim. During a feeding session, a Peeler is in a constant state of ecstasy. The victim will not only adore them but also defend them. They turn normal people into junkies. It only ends when the feeding ends. So when their victim can offer no more they are discarded and the Gläm moves on to someone else.

The hunger that the Gläm feels is also incredibly powerful and they are most vulnerable when they are feeding. Their necessity to feed is linked to an integral process of their evolution. They must have proteins to synthesize the new DNA required to grow and change. The proteins they digest also allow them to extract the genetic information necessary to alter their body structure. This is also why women are preferred as they have the ability to create life. Gläm themselves reproduce asexually and are forbidden to conceive a child as a host. Their offspring are implanted, a gruesome and unnatural form of conception. A show came on TV a couple days ago, about Nightmares of Nature. Apparently, there is a type of Parasitoid wasp that lays its eggs in caterpillars. The eggs hatch inside the caterpillar and the larva consume their host. The odd thing was that the host doesn't just fall over in a heap and die. It will actually keep going right along and even defend the invaders. The larva somehow emits some kind of mind control over their vessel. As vile as the practices of the Gläm seem to us, it would seem that nature has been doing it right along.

The Bobbit Worm was on next. It's the stuff of nightmares. These worms live in burrows in the ocean floor. They can grow up to ten feet long. They have bioluminescent and chemical lures, like the Gläm. They erupt from their burrows to seize prey and pull them underground. A toxin is injected to stun the victim. Then serrated jaws scissor their meal into chunks to be consumed. All the more terrifying is the rumor that some have been reported to grow between 35 and 50 feet in length. Their size is only held in check by the availability of food. Undoubtedly the Gläm are akin to these fiends as so much of their physiology is comparable.

Eels followed the Bobbit worm. Again, there were so many commonalities to the Gläm.

Some eels actually burrow into other living things, not just carcasses. Pearlfish embed themselves in sea cucumbers and live there. Apparently little is known about how eels reproduce despite scientific investigation. Yet the stages of their development appear to be very similar to the Gläm. I may just be viewing all this through the lens of the Servator but if we knew more about the Gläm's origin it may be essential to orchestrating their destruction.

SAVED

Gavin had been thinking a lot lately about his grandmother and how she tried so hard to do right by him. She didn't have much, but she had a work ethic that would put most people to shame. She was the most genuine, most caring person he had ever met. His own mother died when he was young. Gavin's mom was a wonderfully charismatic woman. She had a way of making a room brighter just by walking into it. Her laugh was both melodic and infectious. It was hard to feel down with Maggie Cross around. He could still remember some of their times together, although he had not even started school yet when she passed.

Gavin remembered the last day he saw her well; she had picked him up from daycare, his mother needed to have a chat with Miss Colleen, his teacher; he had gotten into a shoving match with another boy during recess. Gavin liked to play on the swings and somebody stole his turn. He remembered having baked Ziti for lunch. It was a Friday and they were headed to Grandma's house to have pizza and ice cream sundaes. His Dad was supposed to pick up Nathan from school and meet them there. Both the boys loved going to see their Grandmother. Gavin and Nathan were also aware, even at a young age, that if they were having dinner at her place their Dad wouldn't dare show up late or skip it altogether. Grandma was as sweet as could be, but not to be trifled with. She tolerated none of her son's excuses when it came to spending time with family.

Sadly, they never made it to Grandma's that Friday night. They were singing together when they crashed. His mother loved to sing. It was the third round of one of his favorites, *A Hole in the Bottom of the Sea*. They were shouting "There's a frog, there's a frog," as the windshield exploded, spraying glass backwards into the vehicle. A dump truck loaded with gravel from a nearby quarry had pulled out in front of them. His mother had been smiling at him in the rearview mirror. It had been a blessing she did not suffer.

Maggie Cross was killed instantly.

Gavin had no memory of how it happened but somehow he ended up, amid sirens and flashing lights, upright in his car seat sitting outside of the vehicle. It seems that he remembered different versions of that day, some where he and Nathan were together. In some memories he was alone. In others they had hit a deer.

He remembered his Grandma once saying that he was her "little miracle boy." After his mother died he spent a lot of time with his Grandma. One day, she took him to the park to swing and play in the sandbox. He had a Tonka truck front loader and was building pyramids of sand. Another boy joined him and he heard condolences offered to his Grandma as she sat on the bench nearby.

"That little Gav, it's a miracle. Poor Maggie was crushed, and there he was just sitting on the side of the road without a scratch."

He could only figure that was the moment when the two of them became even closer. When things got weird with his Dad, he didn't think twice about who he needed to spend his days with. In the crazy storm that was his life, she was a shining, smiling beacon and she baked the best damn chocolate chip cookies he had ever had to this day.

Gavin had always told himself that he wanted better for his kid. He wanted to be there in ways his dad never was. He didn't know now if he would ever have the chance to be there for Clara. It was funny, he thought, his daughter likes to swing too. Gavin had been staring out the front window of the cabin at an old maple tree, lost in memory. He pulled his hands from his pockets and stepped out the front door, carefully prancing over his improvised alarm wires. It occurred to him that he hated the idea of not being part of Clara's life more than ever dreamed possible. The feeling was a mix of self-loathing but also disappointment. Gavin realized that he was missing out on so many memories and moments. All the times he would never get a chance to have with her, times his own father had missed out on because of the Gläm. His mother, his brother and father, and Uncle John all lost due to their evil influence. It was too overwhelming to process. Gavin told himself, it's better to look forward to having a future with Clara, maybe even Linda, than nothing at all. Things were still too dangerous to be close to his wife and kid, at least for now.

He circled around the back to the tiny shed where Uncle John had kept tools and odd bits of lumber. It didn't take much rummaging before he found a slab of 2 x 10 just under three feet long. Hanging from nails pounded into the frame were lengths of rope. Gavin gathered his materials and circled back out front. Beneath the shade of the maple, he carefully carved two notches at each end of the plank, stringing the lengths of rope from each end and tossed them up and over an outstretched limb. The ropes were slid a bit to adjust for height and then firmly knotted in place. He gently settled on to the swing, testing its sturdiness, and found it was quite strong. Gavin spent the rest of that day until sunset swinging and wondering if he had really been lucky at all the day of his mom's crash.

STALKED

Gavin hopped off the swing as dusk began to settle across the Adirondacks. He gathered up the tools and excess rope and trudged back to the shed. The dirt driveway ended in a cul-de-sac of sorts behind the cabin, with the shed situated across from the back door. The time spent swinging was a welcome catharsis. The act of building it had dredged up some incredibly difficult memories and realizations but actually using it offered solace. Gavin grinned, having experienced a brief moment of satisfaction and peace, as he pulled open the shed doors and stepped inside. Gavin hung the loops of rope back up and put the tools away.

A heavy, hollow-sounding thud banged like thunder against the back of the shed. Gavin spun on his heels and rushed out of the shed to investigate. As he stepped down out of the shed he was pounced on by a mountain lion; it had clearly jumped up onto the roof before leaping down on him as he exited. He went down to the ground hard, its claws tearing open his shoulders. Somehow he had the presence of mind to roll over onto his back despite having the wind knocked out of him. He drove his left forearm into the mouth of the cat. It was in that brief instant that he locked eyes with the animal and knew this wasn't random. An irritated clicking sound was coming from the mouth of the cat and he noticed that its eyes were an icy blue.

Strange things go through your head when you think you're about to die. Perhaps the strangest thought is that you should be dead already.

Gavin couldn't help but think that a mountain lion would have gone right for the throat. Instead, this one simply knocked him down. It was with that thought that a resolve rushed through him he had not known before. He began to use his own arm to gain leverage, first simply pushing back at the beast and then reaching with his other hand grasping the top jaw. He calmly pushed himself up, standing the big cat up on its hind legs. He somehow possessed a poise and strength he was never accustomed to before. He swung himself around and onto the back of the cat, tearing its jaws apart. The Gläm lodged in the back of its throat was now protruding, hanging from the lower jaw. The rasping clicks were now coming in short staccato bursts. Gavin grabbed the cat by its back legs and began smashing its lifeless form against the trunk of a pine to remove the Gläm from his body. He could not understand where the strength was coming from, as though he was a passenger in his own body in that moment. After two solid whacks against the tree the Gläm was ejected from the corpse. Gavin stomped it into the dirt once, twice and a third time for good measure. Certain it was dead, he risked a look back at the cat and noticed that its ribs stood out too sharply and that a plastic neon clip was attached to one of its ears.

He knew at once that somehow they had gotten a hold of this poor creature. That they knew he had been here for some time and they used the poor thing to get rid of him. He knew he had to get in touch with Madson and Becker. First, he had to make sure he cleaned his wounds. He ran to the bathroom, tore off his shirt and began pouring peroxide over both of his shoulders. It was a powerful sting. He tried to steady himself clutching the sink and looked into the mirror. It was then that he realized that his eyes were not his own. Clearly what he saw in the mirror were cat's eyes.

SOUND THE ALARM

Gavin stared at his reflection in the mirror. His pupils had become slits and his eyes were an amber color. His vision was ebbing in and out in concentric waves. He urgently scooped handfuls of cold water from the sink and splashed them on his face. After two or three rounds of cold water, he found his vision had returned to normal. He hurried to his bedside table to retrieve the burner phone that Becker had supplied each of them with. He turned it on and waited for it to find a signal. He texted Becker.

"*Phantasmagoria.*" He waited, stared at the phone for a reply. In less than a minute Becker's reply came through.

"Where?"

"Cabin, need help."

"45 mins."

Gavin powered off the phone and put it back in the drawer. He grabbed the shotgun from the nightstand and went to the living room to wait for their arrival.

* * *

Nathan and Xavier knew the instant their assassin was killed. Nathan had never seen Xavier look quite so thunderstruck. It was utterly evident this was not the expected outcome. Xavier put his head in his hands, he was at a total loss.

"He killed a fucking mountain lion?" Xavier grumbled into his lap.

Nathan had never heard Xavier swear. He wasn't sure if he was in awe of his benefactor cursing or that his brother had somehow not only survived the attack, but killed the predator sent for him.

His ward spoke, not out loud, however Nathan and Xavier heard it clearly. "This confirms a suspicion we have…"

"And…" Xavier asked, clearly irritated.

"The boy was conceived while I was present. He is a Siphon."

"What the hell…" Nathan hadn't finished his question when Xavier sent the desk cartwheeling end over end across the room. It literally flipped and was embedded in the wall. Allura came rushing into the room to see what was going on. Xavier stormed past her, kicking the outer door off its hinges, he roared as he barreled down the hallway.

"A fucking Siphon!"

Nathan couldn't help but chuckle. Twice in one day?

ESCAPADE

Becker motioned to his partner, Madson, to follow him as he got up from his desk. Madson shoved his gorilla-like frame up out of his chair in a futile effort to keep up with his quick and sprightly-moving partner. Becker moved rapidly down the hall and toward the evidence room. The precinct was bustling; he let himself in and nodded to his partner as he closed the door behind him. Madson understood and stood guard at the door. Becker knew exactly where to find what he was looking for; needing to move quickly; grabbed the notes from the now-deceased Dr. Larson and adeptly slid them beneath his blazer. Becker reached a hand in his pocket to hold the bottom of the manilla folder, while keeping it concealed. Popping out of the evidence room so abruptly that he bumped into the broad shoulders of his startled partner. Madson grumbled but did not cry out.

Becker continued moving quickly down and out toward the street-side exit. Once the two of them were across the street, and in the parking lot, Becker told Madson, "We need to get to my house and up to the cabin. It will only take a few moments to load the car."

It was only a matter of minutes to get from downtown Saratoga to Wilton. Becker and his family had a modest raised ranch that had been kept in impeccable condition.

Becker backed his car up to the garage, then sprang out and hit the garage door opener. The garage was neat and clean with little to no clutter. Beside the kitchen entrance, there was a bulkhead leading to a sub-basement. It was padlocked from the outside. Becker undid the lock with a key on his retractable keychain and descended the stairs. He yelled to his partner to back the car into the garage and began piling large black ballistic cases at the top of the stairs.

Madson knew not to ask questions at times like this; his partner's efficiency and tenacity were unparalleled. Many people misjudged his mousey appearance for timidness, but Madson knew all too well that it was just a clever ruse. He slowly and carefully backed the car in and popped the hatch. He struggled to remove himself from the powder blue Prius and began loading the cases into the back of the car. Some were so long that they needed to span the width of the backseat.

Becker finished bringing up the cases that he had deemed necessary; he relocked the bulkhead and hopped into the passenger seat.

"You're not driving?" Madson asked, puzzled.

"No, I have some reading to do," he replied as he slid a manilla folder out from above the driver's side visor.

Madson smirked and awkwardly shoved himself into the

driver's seat. Luckily, he knew where they were going. From where they were in Wilton it was a straight shot up Northern Pines road and past Scotty's Diner to get headed north on I-87. In a short time they were moving and on their way to Gavin.

Becker had already processed nearly half of the documents in the folder by the time they had traveled the fifteen miles from Exit 16 to Exit 20, yet they still had a ways to go. He was a ferocious reader and was in the process of putting sticky notes in various spots when Madson interrupted.

"What have we here?" He gestured, waving his right hand over the folder.

Becker replied, "These are Dr. Larsen's notes on Gavin," as he applied a pink sticky note to the top of a page.

"What good are they?" Madson inquired.

"I think they will help shed some light on how deep this all goes. From what I've read, it would appear that the doctor had been in league with them for quite some time."

Madson got quiet, he gripped the steering wheel forcefully and gritted his teeth.

"What is it?" Becker asked out of concern due to his partner's sudden mood swing.

"I can't help it!" Madson retorted through his clenched teeth.

"I delivered Gavin right to that son of a bitch all those years ago! "

Becker sighed, "You didn't know, none of us knew," and returned to reading as they headed toward North Creek.

Enthralled

* * *

Gavin heard Madson and Becker as they came up the long drive. The road had some gravel in it at one point; it was now mostly loose dirt and rocks here and there. They pulled around back and parked. Gavin could hear them close their doors. Madson was grumbling about something he couldn't quite make out. Madson was already fired up because, before Gavin had a chance to warn him, he was tripped up in fishing line at the front door accompanied by a chorus of tinkling bells.

"Jumpin' Jesus on a pogo stick! What is this, a Salvation Army convention?" Madson was loudly protesting.

"I told you," Becker shouted from the driveway.

Gavin thought to himself that sometimes things remaining the same is a fine comfort.

He put down the shotgun to rescue Madson from his twisted Christmas carol of curses and bells. The big man was struggling with a long ballistic case that was rather heavy. Madson half walked half dragged the case into the cabin.

"Just like old times," Madson grunted.

Gavin went out to the car to see if he could help with anything else only to find Becker gently sliding the dead Gläm into a long cylindrical jar with a rubber grommet and clasp.

"Research," Becker answered Gavin's unasked question without ever turning around.

"I didn't realize you had taken such an interest," Gavin mused.

"I have and I want in." Becker's tone was flat but there was intensity in it.

"You mean you want to be a Servator?"

"I do, very much," Becker's back was still to Gavin as he shifted his attention to examining the mountain lion's remains.

"I haven't finished transcribing my Uncle's book."

"Well, you will just need to hurry up," Becker teased.

Madson was tromping back to the car. "Either one of you gonna give me a hand with this stuff or are you just gonna sit there and poke at dead things for the rest of the night?"

TROUBLE

Allura hurried after Xavier down the hallway. Her long black hair was braided and swung side-to-side as she chased him. One arm still clutched her folio, her other free hand patted the air in the space between her and Xavier in a futile effort to coax him to calm down

Nathan could see her pleading with him down the hall, as the door had been ripped from its hinges during his tantrum. Xavier was shouting and flailing his arms in the hall and Allura wanted to get him someplace more private to try to assess the situation.

"But, Sir," she cajoled, desperately trying to get a word in.

There were brief snippets of him speaking in the Gläms' ancient tongue which was reserved for communicating between Immortals, or moments of duress. Three office staff members hurriedly tried to grab their things and head to the nearest exit but were blocked. Xavier was having a meltdown right in front of the elevator doors. Allura was able to persuade him back into his office. She quietly nodded her head to the frantic staff, their faces were aghast. Allura waved a hand toward the exit. They quickly hustled toward the elevator doors. The fuming giant of a man had now been successfully, and safely, relocated back to his office. Allura was convincing him to sit and relax for a moment.

"Please, Sir." She motioned for him to sit in his chair.

She grabbed her legal pad and pen in order to take notes whilst standing, positioning herself between Xavier and the exit, just in case.

Nathan remained in his chair throughout all of this, it would seem that even his ward was at a loss. He heard no chatter from it and he had thought it best to stay out of Xavier's way.

"Sir, what has happened?"

"Gavin's a fucking Siphon," Xavier snapped

Nathan repressed a chuckle at the F-bomb hat trick. He adjusted himself in his seat to mask his levity.

"And you…" Xavier pointed a long claw-like finger across the space where the desk once was. It was still on-end stuck into the wall.

"*Aie R'Vud. Aie Zyol Vib'Pov'n*" Nathan heard and understood "You knew. You said nothing"

Nathan's Gläm replied internally, "*Sir, the transition from Charles to Nathan stretched a fog across the memory.*"

"It happened decades ago," Xavier shouted.

Allura was nervously tapping her pen, unsure as to what she should actually be writing down. She had never in her years of service seen Xavier behave this way and was not sure how to help in this situation.She usually knew what to do, almost always, but not now. Not with this. These were unexpected matters of an unprecedented variety. Immortals had disagreements over business and territory, Allura had experienced those types of outbursts, but this was beyond that. Somehow, she sensed that the ramifications were more far-reaching than she presently understood.

Xavier stood and turned to the window. He smoothed his blazer in an effort to compose himself, then stared out the window and coolly spoke.

"There is only one way to handle a rogue Siphon." Xavier crossed his arms. "He must be destroyed."

Allura was watching him intently. She nodded in agreement. "Sir, how would you like it handled?"

"Directly and immediately," Xavier's tone implied that this was not negotiable.

"Shall I contact our threat resolution team?"

Xavier nodded silently to confirm. Allura immediately took out her cell phone and placed a call on speakerphone. It rang only once and a gravelly male voice answered.

"Madam, what is the priority level?"

"Highest," Allura glanced at Xavier; he was nodding as he stared out the window.

"The team will be in the parking garage in under ten minutes for briefing." The team leader replied.

"Sir," Allura spoke as she rose from her chair, "I will meet them to deliver instructions."

"I will accompany you," Xavier replied coldly.

"But Sir…" Allura began to speak but Xavier interrupted her.

"I want to accentuate the gravity of the situation to them."

DOCTOR'S NOTES

Becker and Gavin left the corpse of the mountain lion and moved to the car to help Madson unload. There were four more ballistic cases in the trunk and another large one in the back seat. Madson grabbed the larger one despite his struggles with the first one. The four cubes in the back of the car were left for Gavin and Becker. It seemed each one weighed about 40 pounds. Luckily there were handles on either side. It took a couple of trips but they got everything brought inside.

"So, what's this all for?" Gavin asked.

Becker knelt, unlatching the clasps of one of the cubes. He looked over his shoulder at Gavin with a puzzled look.

"Perimeter defense." His response implied that the answer ought to have been obvious.

"What do you mean?" Gavin's tone was worried.

"What he means," Madson interjected, "is that they know where you are and they are coming."

Gavin's head began to spin a little bit. His eyes must have conveyed the message to Becker. He rose from one knee and gently guided Gavin to a chair. Becker sat him down and in a quiet, almost fatherly, manner began to explain.

"We agreed that this place was remote enough that bystanders would not be involved. Our hope had been that it would take longer for them to discover you were staying here. Unfortunately, that is not the case. I have brought provisions to help secure this location and we are going to be putting them in place." Becker paused for a moment and put his hand on Gavin's shoulder. "Does that make sense?" Becker calmly waited for Gavin to respond.

Gavin nodded in quiet agreement.

Madson walked over to the table and stood beside Becker. The very same old kitchen table where Gavin and his Uncle John formulated their plans to rescue Nathan, to no avail.

"Listen bud," Madson started clearing his throat before he continued. "Beck and I talked this through on the way up here. We think the best thing to do is to give them a hell of a fight up here away from everyone and everything. None of us want our families getting sucked into this."

Madson realized too late what he had said. He had not intended to wound Gavin with his words but he had, he could see it in his face.

"I'm sorry, Gavin," Madson rubbed his hand on the back of his head. "I know they already got to your folks, but think about your wife and kid. We need to make sure that our wives and kids are kept clear of all this."

Gavin knew he was right, but that didn't keep it from stinging. It was a hard truth but it was a good plan.

Gavin stood up, shook his head a bit, and clapped his hands together, rubbing them briskly.

"Okay then," he exhaled loudly, "Well, what have we got here?"

Gavin walked over to the cases lined up on the floor. Madson and Becker simply nodded to each other and walked over to join him.

Before Gavin could even get into any of the cases, Becker proposed a different task. "I actually have some information that may be of interest to you," Becker offered, handing a folder to Gavin. "I took the liberty of printing out a copy of some of the notes that Dr. Larson had compiled in regard to your sessions."

"I guess I didn't realize he kept notes," Gavin stated, taking the folder from Becker.

"It would seem that the good doctor was keeping tabs on a number of his patients." Becker raised his eyebrows disdainfully. "If he hadn't crashed his vehicle and perished he would have lost his license due to some of his extracurricular activities."

"Really?" Gavin was genuinely flabbergasted.

"I put a pink post-it note on one file that seemed rather peculiar." Becker pointed to the spot and returned to unload the cases.

Gavin plopped down into a chair with the folder and opened to the marked set of notes. Before he could begin to read Becker added another comment.

"I noticed the tag on the ear of the mountain lion."

"Yeah," Madson chimed in, "What the hell happened with that?"

Gavin grew quiet. He wasn't sure how to respond. "I killed it," he said absently as he started to read.

From the date at the top Gavin guessed that he must've been about 15 years old when these notes were taken. His visits with Dr. Larson were a necessity after the evening he experienced his father feeding on a Peeler. His father had tried to play it off as a boy walking in on a moment of intimacy but Gavin saw what was really happening. His guts twisted with a cold, sick feeling as he realized how long they had been scrutinizing him through Dr. Larson. He was also put "under" for hypnosis fairly regularly and couldn't help but wonder what the Doctor had been up to. At times, he found his memories were unreliable, as though there were different versions of the events he experienced. According to the notes, Dr. Larson believed that many of his current struggles were based upon that single traumatic event. He also implied that Gavin's feeling of agoraphobia and somewhat histrionic reactions to events were attempts at finding control. All the while the doctor was angling to get into the Gläm's super-secret club. The doctor's animosity toward Gavin must have reached a boiling point and he decided to try some experimental therapy. The doctor often would refer to it as hide and seek; Gavin remembered it now that he started to read the notes. The exercise was one they did a number of times. Gavin had naïvely believed that it was done in an effort to make him more comfortable in crowds on the city street. The notes he was reading now suggested that the activity was intended to overwhelm Gavin and then record his reaction. Gavin wondered just what kind of reaction he was going for. Toward the end of the page written diagonally in sprawling cursive was a note with an arrow that pointed to turn the page over. On the back in the same handwriting, Dr. Larson's, he presumed, was a note:

"When I caught him this time there *was* a change in his eyes."

ANTIQUUS LIBELLUS
SERVATOR JOHN THOMAS

I was watching an Antiques Roadshow the other day and there was a painting of Dionysus or Bacchus that they were examining. For some reason it piqued my interest so I decided to do a little research. The stories of Dionysus seem to be both ordinary and extraordinary. He apparently was one of the many children of Zeus. Zeus fathered many children much to Hera's dismay. Hera wanted to destroy his progeny from his affair. So to save Dionysus, Zeus somehow sewed him into his own thigh. As gruesome as it sounds Hera sought to destroy the mother while she was still pregnant and Zeus removed the child and inserted him into his own body. The part that really got my wheels spinning was that Dionysus seemed to have the ability to control the moods of people and seemed to always somehow have a hand in various kingdoms' royalty. He was considered the god of wine and fertility but also of rage. It was said his abilities spoke of the duality of wine, the ecstasy and the destruction that went with consumption. I can't help but wonder if he was a product of the Gläm. His origins and powers sound a great deal like a human fathered by an Immortal Gläm or one in transition. I was told they are called Siphons. Siphons often exhibit various abilities of the Gläm. Some

Enthralled

can mesmerize, some have telepathic abilities and others can leech the life force from other living things. According to one legend, Dionysus sought revenge and whipped a group of women into a frenzy to a point that they tore men limb from limb. The maenads of Dionysus tore apart Orpheus during his sorrowful laments at the loss of Euridyce, Orpheus himself may have been fathered by the Gläm. He was said to have the ability to mesmerize any living thing with his songs. He also had the gift of prophecy. His remains were kept as relics in the oracles' temples. To put it plainly, I think many myths are metaphors but to me this one sounds like Glämwere involved. Think about how many folk heroes and tall tales could have been the result of the Gläm, they could have been Siphons.

TRY OUT

Madson and Becker were talking amongst themselves as they unpacked the contents of the ballistic cases. Gavin was lost in thought reading the notes from one of his sessions with Dr. Larson. Gavin was distraught; he knew that his memories were all mixed up. It seemed obvious that for some reason the doctor wanted to rearrange events from his past. He was trying hard to put things in order inside his head. It troubled him to his core that such important memories of his loved ones, especially those who passed, were in such disarray. He couldn't shake the feeling that he had to get things sorted, out of respect for his mom and grandma. Gavin wasn't sure how much time had passed but at some point his comrades had finished unpacking the cases. Becker came over to him slowly and began to speak.

"How are you doing, buddy?"

Gavin wasn't really sure how to reply; he just looked up at Becker from his seat. His eyes clearly conveyed that he was lost.

"It's a lot to take in," Becker consoled him. "I read the files on the drive up." He shook his head in his bird-like manner. "The doctor was in league with them from the beginning. None of us on the force would have ever allowed him to be appointed to help you or anyone else had we known."

Madson grunted in affirmation, too emotional to interject.

"I know," Gavin reassured him. "Nobody knew... Wait a second. You read the whole folder on the way up?"

"I read very fast," Becker responded nonchalantly. "I've also gone through some of your uncle's notes and I think I have a theory as to how you survived the attack with the mountain lion."

Gavin was downright amazed. He couldn't fathom how Becker was able to power through documents with such speed.

"Really?" Gavin was curious but also apprehensive.

"I found some sections in your uncle's notes that refer to a phenomenon where a Gläm fathers a child with a woman. The child produced from that union is referred to as a Siphon. These children exhibit abilities that the Gläm possess while retaining their humanity."

Suddenly in Gavin's mind it seemed like things were coming together. He remembered seeing in the mirror how his own eyes had changed in the encounter with the big cat. He had no idea how he was able to overpower it. It just sort of happened, like an instinctual response kicked in. Then there was the note. Dr. Larson had written that there was a change in his eyes.

"So, you think I'm one of them?" Gavin directed his question at Becker.

Madson had by then trundled over to join the conversation.

"No, not a Gläm, but perhaps a Siphor.." Becker was searching Gavin's face to establish his reaction.

"So, my Dad," Gavin paused before continuing. He was doing the math in his head to figure out if his father's age at the time of death and his own birth fit the equation. "He mus-'ve been a host when my mom had me," Gavin declared to his companions.

"It would seem that is the case," Becker added contently, pleased that the discovery hadn't sent Gavin over the edge.

"So, what does that even mean," Gavin asked.

"My theory is that your adrenaline and the dire nature of the attack brought out this ability," Becker spoke to Gavin in a parental tone as if explaining how to make an omelet.

Madson rubbed his head, at a loss for words, or perhaps comprehension.

"Listen," Becker patted Gavin's shoulder. "Time is of the essence, no doubt there are forces heading this way to do you in. What they don't know is that we are here." Becker motioned with his thumb to himself and Madson. "I'd like to use that to our advantage. So, Madson and I are going to go get this stuff set up around the cabin. You might want to take a half an hour or so to make sense of what we've just discovered. Maybe even figure out if we can use your abilities to our advantage. We're going to need everything at our disposal to make it through the night."

Gavin looked overwhelmed. Becker was right, of course. Time was a critical factor. Becker gently urged Gavin out of his chair and began guiding him to the back door. Becker opened the door and led Gavin out. He left him at the cul-de-sac, puzzled, but instilled with purpose. Becker turned away from Gavin and headed inside.

As he entered he yelled to Gavin, "Think of it as a tryout."

BRIEFING

Nathan stood quietly in the background, his hands folded behind his back, near the elevator doors. Xavier and Allura stood side by side in front of him as the van pulled to a stop. The van was comically disguised as an extermination service called *Pest Erase*. It would seem that humor was not forsaken on the Gläm, or perhaps coincidentally they found this vehicle at auction and deemed it pleasing. In many ways, it was fitting and spoke to the matter at hand.

The orange and black van's windows were tinted, making it especially difficult to see inside given the dim lighting on this level of the parking garage. The driver and passenger doors opened simultaneously, followed by the sliding panel door. Five men in full black tactical gear emerged. Each of them was over six feet tall, well built, and carried automatic rifles with sidearms strapped to their thighs.

Allura and Xavier walked forward to meet with the team as they efficiently formed themselves into a semicircle to receive their orders. As Xavier strode forward, outdistancing Allura with his longer determined strides, the team leader took one step forward from the middle of the group.

"Sir." Nathan recognized the voice from Allura's phone call earlier.

Xavier came to an abrupt stop inches from the man's face. Each member of the team was tall but Xavier still towered over them.

"I very much need you to understand one thing," Xavier held up one finger. "This needs to be dealt with flawlessly. Get rid of him and burn the whole damn place to the ground. I expect confirmation of this before six tomorrow morning. Is that clear?"

"Yes, Sir," The team leader responded, his team nodded in solemn agreement. Allura stepped forward and handed the team leader a sealed manila envelope. Inside were photos of Gavin, John's cabin, a topographical map of the area, and the cabin's GPS coordinates and address. He took the envelope with a quick bow, and he and his team turned on their heels and loaded back into the van.

Allura and Xavier spun in unison and moved back to the elevator. Nathan joined them and all three of them stepped through the doors as they opened in silence. Only once the doors had closed did Xavier speak to them.

"We need to sit down and talk this out," Xavier said in nearly a whisper while rubbing his temples.

"Sir," Allura's tone was timid, "may I suggest a few moments to rest."

Xavier chuckled, "My dear, I will rest far better when this issue is resolved."

Allura nodded and spoke no more of it. Nathan's curiosity got the better of him.

"Is the issue not resolved? What is it that we need to discuss?"

Xavier let out a long contemptuous sigh, "Your brother."

Nathan did not say another word for the remainder of the elevator ride. When they returned to Xavier's office the door had been fixed and the desk put back in place, though a hole remained in the wall as a reminder of where the desk had been lodged. Xavier sat behind the desk and Allura and Nathan sat down across from him. Allura readied herself to take notes. An office staff member quickly and quietly wheeled in a cart with a bucket of iced bottled water and then vanished. Once she had gone and the door closed behind her, Xavier kicked his feet up on the desk and reclined. He closed his eyes and stretched his arms upward. He then laced his fingers together behind his head and sighed before getting started.

"Nathan, how old is your brother?"

ANTIQUUS LIBELLUS SERVATOR JOHN THOMAS

My brain started racing to make connections after digging around to find out more about Bacchus. It is purely conjecture but I think one could break it down by looking at the powers that we are aware the Gläm possess. From what I have read from my predecessor Bobby and what I have witnessed myself I think there are three to four Gläm abilities.

The first would be the ability to mesmerize or captivate a victim. As far as I can tell most advanced Gläm have very crystal clear blue eyes. I have heard that the ability is related to bioluminescence often found in the deep sea. When they are attempting to control someone a pale blue glow emanates from their eyes. In a well lit setting it is imperceptible but in the dark it can be seen clearly. The power of suggestion or mind manipulation pops up in myriad tales throughout time. Even those figures from history said to ooze charisma may be a result of the Gläm. The Pied Piper captivated people and animals. The Sirens call lured sailors to their doom. The Satori were said to know your thoughts before you did. Nymphs and Fae folk charmed passersby. There are undoubtedly far more.

The second ability is similar to their manipulative gaze. Gläm can speak telepathically to one another. They can also utilize a twisted empathic talent.

I am uncertain as to how they are able to communicate in such a way. It may be due to the fact they are all essentially a part of the same whole. They share perception and experiences and are aware of each other. It may also be that they project their strange clicks and clacks at a decibel level humans can't process. The fact that they share some sort of hive-mind may also mean that they are more connected than we previously considered. Perhaps they are linked to some sort of original or creator being. They also seem to have the power of suggestion. They can affect people through the secretion of subtle pheromones; they are able to woo people and create a mood in confined spaces. One Immortal Gläm could make a room of people happy or sad, horny or timid.

A third power is tied to their need to consume. A Gläm must feed to evolve. The Gläm grow more powerful as they grow and change. Eating proteins allows them to not only satiate hunger but also extract and synthesize DNA which is then woven into them. This leeching or vampirism necessitates prey. They feed on us to become more like us and in time become "better" or beyond us. In applying this ability to Siphons they could similarly leech from living things. Think of all the great heroes who overpowered beasts in their quests. They may have been using the strength they sapped from the creatures they defeated. Hercules and the Nemean Lion may have been one such instance. He even made a cloak from it, maybe to continually draw power from it. Cuchulain fought the Hound of Ulster and "became" the hound. Even our own beloved Adirondack hero Paul Bunyan had Babe the Blue Ox, always at his side. My thought would be that the theory wouldn't only apply to strength but also tales of shapeshifters, werewolves and magical familiars. So many figures from legend had constant animal companions.

The stories passed down of Witches and their familiars may also indicate a deeper and more disturbing aspect of the Gläm. The familiar, or animal

51

consort, of the Witch may have been a source of their abilities as Siphons. Far more despicable may be that the Gläm orchestrated Witch trials and even the Inquisition in an attempt to remove their half-breed transgressions. None the less they always weasel their way into positions of power. Regardless they no doubt used the atrocities as a food source.

Another facet of the Gläms' DNA manipulation is that they heal quickly. Those acting as hosts share this boon. Immortals possess regenerative capabilities that make them incredibly hard to destroy. Again, these traits could be passed on to their hybrid offspring. So many tales glorify the invincible character. Achilles was nearly invulnerable. Antaeus was restored each time he touched the earth. Sigurd and the Dragon, Gilgamesh and Enkidu, Beowulf and Grendel even perhaps the Green Knight may be inspired by Gläm involvement.

I realize how far reaching all this sounds. Yet the Servators have chronicled that the Gläm were spread throughout the globe long ago, their offspring would be as well.

REVELATIONS

Nathan paused for a moment. He took a second to do the math in his head. "Twenty-five or twenty-six, maybe."

Xavier groaned in disapproval and sat up in his chair.

"It just doesn't add up," Xavier snapped.

"I guess I'm not sure what isn't adding up," Nathan responded hesitantly.

"Your brother," Xavier replied, perplexed. "How could he be a Siphon, he's too old." Xavier was irritated, there was some piece he was missing. Some part of all of this had been overlooked. Then it dawned on him. Nathan saw his eyes get wide and in an instant Xavier had snatched Nathan from his seat and was holding him aloft. Nathan's feet dangled above the ground. Xavier leaned in close and spoke.

"D'pyb Oz Ob B'pyb Aie Y'u Polov'n M'Yit Tu" What is it that you are hiding from me?

Nathan felt an overwhelming sense of dread. He could feel

how uneasy the Gläm he hosted was, it was shivering inside of him. The Gläm began to speak telepathically to Xavier, *"Sir."*

Xavier cut him off before he could continue, "Out loud so we all can hear."

"If you insist," the voice was coming from Nathan but it wasn't his own. It had a raspy and nasally quality to its sound. *"What we hid from you was only done so to avoid conflict. My former host and I thought it best to ensure transition."*

Xavier lowered Nathan back into his seat. "Go on," he urged as he slid back down in his own chair.

"Our fear was that if it was known, turmoil would ensue amongst our ranks."

"If what was known?" Xavier's patience had dwindled.

"That one of your Immortal brothers forced himself upon the Cross woman."

Xavier shot back in his seat, his expression thunderstruck. "Which one was it?"

"Xavier, it happened so long ago. I only know because I was able to peer through the veil that clouded it from my host's memories. It happened early on in the recruitment of Charles; I was still connected to his father at that point. We were planning the transition to Charles when it happened. There had been a party in town. Many of our kind were present in an effort to coax Charles into accepting. They were at the bar and it was getting late. He and Maggie were getting ready to leave. They walked to the coat check when some men grabbed Charles and began chatting him up. When he turned back he found that his wife was missing. He was frantic and began searching for her only to discover she had been dragged into the

coat room. A man was forcing himself upon her. Charles grabbed him to pull him off. It was then he realized who it was, but he and his wife would have no memories of any of this. They were charmed by the attacker."

"Who was it?" Xavier growled.

"It was Oni."

"Oni," Xavier was even more perplexed now that he had gotten an answer.

READINESS

Gavin was all mixed up. A flood of mismatched and evidently manipulated memories poured into his head. It was like a levy broke once he read the session notes from Dr. Larson. Now Becker expected him to walk it off and prepare for whatever was coming next. Suddenly, he became aware that he had, somehow, subconsciously moved towards the shed. There the pitiful body of the cougar lay in a heap. He hadn't really thought about what should be done with the remains. Even though it had tried to kill him, it was essentially a puppet. Gavin still felt bad about it. It really was a beautiful creature, a little underweight but still a marvel. Kneeling down beside it, absentmindedly stroking the fur behind its front legs, running a hand across its ribs. In that brief moment, Gavin felt a sensation akin to magnetism. Similar to when someone is holding two magnets and inertia breaks and they are drawn together. Gavin's hand began to pulse. His palm pumped like a piston on the cat's side, though quite startled, unable to break from the trance ensuing. Gavin was vaguely aware that Becker and Madson had come out the door. Both men had armloads of gear. Something in the way Gavin was poised alarmed them. They carefully put the equipment by the back door and slowly walked toward him, calling out tentatively.

"Gav," Becker spoke gently while inching closer. "You okay?"

Becker reached out to pat Gavin's shoulder. Madson was a full two steps behind. An instant before Becker made contact, Gavin simply erupted from his crouch and leapt nearly twelve feet in the air. He flew up and through branches into a pine and landed on a thick outstretched branch, perched to face the two men as a shower of branches and pine needles fell. Madson reflexively drew his sidearm. Becker slowly stood up straight and walked backward, his right arm aloft silently pleading with his partner to put the gun down.

"Put it down," Becker whispered without looking back. Madson lowered his weapon.

"What the hell just happened?" Madson hoarsely grumbled back.

Becker was still intently watching Gavin. He looked as though he was about to pounce on the two of them. Becker tried to softly speak to him in an effort to avoid any unfortunate events.

"Gavin, hey it's just me and Madson. There's no need to be afraid."

Becker stepped backward alongside his partner. He motioned with his hand to holster the gun. Madson made a sound like a bullfrog; if they were words only he knew their meaning. Yet he complied and Becker spoke to Gavin.

"Look, the gun is away. Why don't you come down and we

can help sort this out."

Gavin could hear the words but it was as though they were being played on a distant radio. The two men in front of him were familiar but his vision made it hard to realize. It was as though he was seeing them as an old movie. Colors were nearly gone and grayscale had taken over his sight. The stark difference between what he knew vision to be and this was unsettling. As his heart began to slow down he was able to hear them better, more clearly. He hopped down and tried to brush himself off. His hair was full of pine needles and he shook his head to dislodge them.

"Sorry," he nearly purred the phrase. The sound of his altered speech made him chuckle. His giggle helped to break the tension.

Becker wiped the sweat off his brow with the back of his hand. He declared, "Gavin, you just scared the shit out of me!"

The comment made Gavin laugh out loud. Becker joined in as well, the two of them nearly in tears. The joke must've been lost on Madson, he found no humor in it. So he reiterated his previous question. "What the hell just happened?"

SIEGE

The exterminator van snaked through Manhattan and made it out onto I-87. It would've normally taken them about three or four hours to get from the city to the Adirondacks, yet rush hour would be against them. Ultimately it would have the team of trained killers arriving in the dead of night. The cover of darkness would work to their advantage once they arrived and were on foot. If they were discreet in navigating the small county roads of North Creek it would help them arrive unannounced. Despite how skilled the mercenaries were they would still need to drive with their headlights on to get into position to surround the cabin.

The traffic would slow them down, giving Gavin, Becker and Madson time to prepare. If there was one thing Becker prided himself on, it was being prepared. Although foresight for him had been a challenge ever since the death of Charles Cross, it had been a rapidly changing series of unexpected events ever since. Planning for such supernatural matters as these had never crossed his mind.

* * *

"Never a dull moment," Becker chortled.

"How did you...." Madson stammered, turning toward Becker, " How did he?"

Becker wrapped an arm around his partner. "It's easier to just roll with it than to figure it out." The two men moved to the back door of the cabin. They picked up the cases where they had set them down.

"We don't have time to figure it out anyway," Becker giggled. "I do think we can use it though. Whoever is coming doesn't know we are here." Becker motioned to his partner and himself. He then pointed to Gavin, "They also don't know that you can do that." Becker began moving into the tree line with one of the cases. Madson had already grabbed a case and was following Becker. Gavin picked one up as well and yelled, "So, what's in the cases?"

Becker turned around and gave a smug grin, "They don't know about these either."

He motioned for the other two men to follow him. A worn and small trail led up a gentle slope. The cabin sat in a bowl shaped parcel of land. Boulders and pines ringed the edge of the lot. The three of them proceeded to place trail cams around the area along trails and deer runs as well as four Claymore anti-personnel mines. An additional trail cam was placed near the mailbox. Becker did not believe that anyone would drive directly up to the cabin. He was hoping that they would drive by to scout it out and thereby also alert them to their presence. Becker had the trail cams set up to view from his laptop. The Claymores were set up with trip wires and an ingenious tactic to ensure efficacy. Just beyond each trip wire on the side closer to the cabin and down slope sticks were placed in overlapping V shapes. If the wires were detected and stepped over the sticks were placed on rock or log fulcrums to trigger detonation. Now that everything was in place Becker needed to present the plan to his cohorts. It was getting darker by the minute and they needed to be ready. He urged them to sit at the kitchen table to discuss the scenario.

"Okay." He slid a box of matches while speaking. "Here's the cabin and here's the shed." He put a pepper shaker in place of the shed. "I'm banking on them not coming right up to the house via the driveway." He traced a route with his finger from the edge of the table to the box of matches. "I'm thinking that they'll case the joint first then move in through the woods."

"Why do you think they'd do that?" Gavin asked absentmindedly, running his index finger along the side of the table.

"Because that's what I'd do." Becker continued on, "When the trail cams pick up movement we're going to fire flares from the windows." He picked wooden matches from his palm and put them down to indicate the trail cams. "They'll likely be using night vision, the flares will blind them long enough to pick them off with these." Becker motioned to the high powered rifles equipped with suppressors resting on the kitchen chairs. "We don't know how many are coming, which could be problematic. Do you think you could handle some reconnaissance in the trees using the new trick you learned?" Becker paused waiting for Gavin's reply.

"Uh, sure. What's the worst that could happen?" Gavin scratched his head looking at the table blankly.

Enthralled

"You could die, we could all die. That's the worst that could happen." Madson blurted out the obvious.

* * *

Gavin was trying to psych himself up. It was dark and Madson was holding the flashlight for him. He watched the pocket knife in his hand shake in the light. He felt compelled to act, but queasy at the same time. Something inside of him told him he needed to do this but he was hesitant.

"Just get it over with," Madson grumbled. "We're running out of time."

Gavin exhaled heavily in acknowledgment. He grasped one of the front claws of the mountain lion between his thumb and index fingers and cut it off at the base. Madson abruptly clicked off the light and shambled back inside. Gavin stood motionless for a moment looking at the claw in his hand. He wasn't sure how it worked but when he touched the dead cat he had changed. Even though it wasn't living any longer, it was as if he needed a catalyst to tap into the energy. Initially when he was attacked by the shed the change came quickly. The second time he focused on the animal and, while touching it, he had changed. Instinctually he knew he needed an aspect or talisman of some kind to make it work again. He followed Madson back into the kitchen and began rummaging around in the junk drawer. Sure enough, he found a single boot lace and an old wire-wrapped top from a champagne bottle. He was able to secure the claw in the wire and create a makeshift necklace for himself. Oddly he remembered his father once recounting at a family get-together that the "thingy" on the top of the champagne bottle was called a muselet from the French "to muzzle" so that the contents would not explode from pressure. He hadn't figured out how to handle the pressure of his father's misdeeds or his death, for that matter. One thing was for certain, Gavin would need to figure out how to unleash his father's curse if he wanted to see tomorrow.

"We got one!" Becker shouted from behind his computer screen. "Panel van just stopped at the mailbox. Kill the lights and get in position."

QUESTIONS

"Oni?" Xavier was still rattled by the discovery that one of his brothers had transgressed so blatantly. Oni was not impulsive. He was calculating, patient and probably one of the most considerate of the Immortals in adhering to decorum. There simply had to be more to it than sheer lust.

"You are certain of this?" Xavier asked, hoping for a crack in the story. Any wavering could mean that there may be a different violator. Perhaps the veil confused the memory of whom it had been.

"I am certain." The Gläm spoke assuredly.

Xavier bolted up from his chair toppling it over. "Out!" He pounded his fist on the desk. "All of you out!"

Allura and Nathan immediately rose and scurried out the door. Allura quietly pulled the door closed behind them and ushered Nathan into an adjoining copy room. Nathan was lost in all of this. His Gläm had just absolutely opened a can of worms decades in the making. Nathan had no idea what any of this meant. Yet one thing had been certain from the conversation, Gavin was not his Father's child. He wasn't Nathan's brother, half-brother it would seem.

"What the hell is going on?" Allura's harsh whisper snapped Nathan out of his pondering. "Is this some kind of game? What are you trying to accomplish here?"

"I have no agenda, I only sought to shed light on the situation." Nathan's Gläm pleaded with her.

"Yet you told no one all these years?" Her tone was skeptical.

"I only wanted to keep my host and his family safe."

"And conveniently yourself as well!" With that Allura stormed out of the copy room, slamming the door behind her. She then barged into her own office and slammed that door shut for good measure. Nathan was left alone in the copy room. He and his ward were left leaning against the copier in awkward silence. He had agreed to become a host with the promise of luxury, extravagance, new territories to claim and rule over and near immortality. Yet here he was in a copy room burned and disfigured, possibly forever, and embroiled in a drama he had no knowledge of or stake in. He found himself forced to converse with his intimate companion. One would think a sentient being lodged within your person would be the first to go talk to. Nathan realized that since this all started he rarely spoke to his Gläm.

Now what? He asked internally.

I really have no idea.

Do we try to talk to them?

I believe that would be a poor choice.

Enthralled

Agreed. Then what do we do?

I could use a snack

I could use a drink. Nathan chuckled after the thought.

Sounds like a plan.

Nathan headed toward the elevators. He took them down to the lobby where he was greeted by a concierge the size of a Grizzly bear.

"Could I get a ride to the club please?"

"Of course sir, a car will be out front momentarily." The mountain of a man bowed.

Nathan strolled out to the curb and waited. Within seconds a black SUV with tinted windows rolled to stop in front of him. The driver hopped out of the vehicle and circled around the front to open the door for him. He closed the door once Nathan was seated and returned to the driver's seat. Lucky for Nathan he could converse with his ward privately as they made their way to Club Decadence.

So what do I call you?

Silence reigned for a moment.

I don't know, I'm both your father and grandfather but also Gläm.

Oh, I just thought I'd ask…" Nathan felt uncomfortable and silly.

No one has ever asked before.

Really, Nathan was genuinely surprised. *My dad never asked?*

Nor your grandfather.

Well, what would you like me to call you?

It was silent again for a moment. *Leto.*

Leto it is then. Nathan smiled, *Leto let's hit the club.*

CONCEALMENT

Gavin was alarmed when he heard Becker call out. They had gone over the plan. Gavin knew his role in it all. He was to move halfway up into the tree line and then having used his newfound abilities to jump high to a perch in the trees. Becker thought it best to have him work the area behind the shed to avoid getting hurt by friendly fire. He clutched the claw talisman he had crafted moments before, hoping it would hold together at least for tonight.

"Let's go," Becker urged from the living room. "Move, move, move..."

Gavin hurried out the back door, across the gravel driveway, and whipped around to the back of the shed. He sank to one knee and, while grasping the claw in both hands, tried to focus on the experience of the animal attacking him. His breathing quickened. A throbbing pulse grew in his palms and in a matter of seconds, his vision shifted into hues of gray scattering the darkness of the night. He spun toward the forest and bolted for the trees. About 30 yards went by in a flash and he found an immense old pine to take position in. As he began to climb, he realized that his own hands had begun to change. His palms and fingers were curved at an angle and his nails had become claw-like. Once safely perched nearly 20 feet up onto a thick outstretched limb he tested his claws. As he curled his fingers forward and back his nails, which had significantly thickened to a point, extended and retracted. Gavin was fascinated but he would need to stay focused. He tried to quiet himself, his breathing and movement, he needed to be still and remain hidden.

Madson and Becker were intently watching the trail cams for movement. Within minutes they saw armed men hustling one by one into position around the perimeter of the property. Men in black tactical gear and equipped with night vision goggles and automatic weapons.rushed to five separate points and crouched, awaiting the signal to move in. From the display on his laptop, Becker could not make out the location of the van. He was not sure if there was someone remaining in the van but that would have to be handled after the five assailants surrounding the cabin were dealt with. He was too transfixed on the screen to try and discern which of them was in charge. Then he saw one of them raise his wrist to his mouth and the other four put their hands to their ears. He now knew which one to take out first and he moved into position at the kitchen window to try and eliminate the leader of the group to further dismantle and confuse their efforts. His scope made everything shades of gray-green but he was able to dial in the distance and lock his crosshair on the crouching figure. His target was nestled beside a pine tree. Becker exhaled slowly and squeezed the trigger.

CONVERSATION

Xavier had been staring at his phone. He'd been running scenarios through his head and simply couldn't fathom what would've motivated Oni, one of his most trusted Immortal brothers, to have committed such an egregious act. What worried Xavier most was that Oni was the farthest thing from impulsive. He was calculating, quiet and in control. So the question became why he did it and to what end. Another odd consideration was how to proceed. An accusation could set things in motion with calamitous consequences. Too coy an inquiry could allow for the scenario to be spun around. Did one call or text or simply show up in a matter such as this? An unannounced appearance was out of the question. Xavier was unaccustomed to self-doubt, his routine was giving orders and making decisions. Second-guessing the machinations of another in his same position was infuriating. Flustered, he snatched up the phone and began to text.

-We need to talk

His index finger hovered over the send button. He covered his eyes with the other hand and pressed send. The two-and-a-half minutes that passed before a response came dragged on for an eternity.

-Of course.

The response only further exasperated Xavier. It was typical of Oni, he could almost hear him saying it. It was simultaneously agreeable and infuriating. It immediately twisted it back on him. Xavier took a deep breath and decided to respond in turn.

-At your earliest convenience.

He waited again for a reply. This one came much quicker.

-The club?

Xavier couldn't decide if he wanted to bite. The club was neutral territory. Yet if Oni selected the location, should it be trusted? Xavier thought that if he could control the time chosen it would determine how much time either of them would have to prepare.

-When?

Xavier watched and waited for a reply.

-Midnight.

Xavier was hoping for sooner. It at least would mean that they both had the same amount of time to prepare. It would have to do.

-Perfect.

IN THE CLUB

Nathan rolled up to the club and was met by a doorman clad in black. The doorman waited for the vehicle to come to a stop and opened the door. Nathan was ushered past all of the Peelers, the Gläm's willing food source, waiting in line. As was customary, they were being checked over thoroughly by two large men at the door. Gläm did not like to dine on contaminated meals. Once inside the dimly lit club, Nathan was escorted to a private room. He would love a stiff drink but alcohol was off-limits to those who hosted a Gläm. Each room was equipped with a call button to request service. Nathan found it resting on the arm of the overstuffed loveseat as usual. He sat and wondered what beverage he could indulge in.

Leto, he was not accustomed to his ward's name yet. *Would a seltzer be alright?*

Oh, very much so, I find the bubbles exhilarating.

Nathan pressed the call button. A polite knock came on the door soon after and his server entered. She walked to the front of the sofa and kneeled with her head bowed.

"Good evening. How may I be of service?"

Nathan scoffed, "Please stand up, that's not necessary."

She quickly rose to her feet and smoothed out her miniskirt with her shaking hands. "Sorry," she stammered. "I was told to greet…"

"Yes, yes," Nathan cooed. "You're new here. I've never seen you before. What is your name?"

"I'm Darla."

"Pleasure to meet you, Darla. I'm Nathan and this is my partner, Leto."

Darla looked absolutely baffled. She really hadn't a clue what was going on, yet she smiled through it and that did wonders for Nathan's spirits. His day had been rough and sometimes one needed a good chuckle. Nathan laughed aloud and proceeded to order.

"I'd like a tall black cherry seltzer on ice with a straw and my companion will take tonight's special."

Confusion reigned on poor Darla's face. She smiled still and shuffled out the door, closing it behind her. Nathan and Leto shared a fit of giggles until her return. They caught themselves when they heard a knock and tried to compose themselves like two schoolboys caught at some prank. Darla had a small round bar tray with Nathan's seltzer which she placed on the low table beside him. Behind her, a tall, curvaceous brunette with her head half-shaved waited for Darla to turn and leave. As soon as the door closed behind Darla the young woman straddled Nathan and began ripping her own top off. Nathan raised his index finger in her face in a gesture to give him a moment. He reached for his seltzer and took two long sips. He placed it back and then flopped back on the loveseat, his arms spread across its back. The Peeler buried his face in her ample breasts and wrapped her arms around his head. The instant Leto began feeding she groaned in ecstasy, writhing her hips against Nathan. Despite the insipid clicking of Leto's jaws, Nathan was rather enjoying himself. It would seem that his day would turn around after all. Once sated, Leto withdrew and Nathan shoved the rag doll aside into the seat next to him. He pushed the call button. Two large men entered in moments to remove the brunette. As they exited Nathan watched them leave with her, and before the door closed three more men entered. Through the haze after feeding Nathan recognized the man standing in the center of them. It was Oni.

Oh, shit, Leto blurted out, exactly just what Nathan had been thinking.

ANTIQUUS LIBELLUS
SERVATOR JOHN THOMAS

On Talismans and Siphons

In doing my research I was not able to pinpoint direct references to Siphons. It would seem that it was easier for people to believe that their local legends and or varied belief structures are to be credited for their extraordinary abilities. It would also make sense that the secretive nature of the Gläm would have also kept the origins of these characters throughout history under wraps. I would gather the Gläm were aware of these figures and were out to destroy them. In thinking about the tales that come to mind I can't help but recollect that they were beleaguered by trials and tribulations. For instance, when we think of Hercules who was said to have always worn the hide of the Nemean lion, he is remembered for his many labors and battles. Perhaps forces sought to destroy him at the request of the Gläm. The Hydra may have been more than just hyperbole given the Gläms' involvement.

My thoughts on the matter keep drifting to Native Americans. Bobby, my predecessor, said that his people knew of the Gläm. They called them Wendigo or Vendol and witnessed their arrival during a Viking encampment. Yet there are so many instances in which a Siphon may be at the center of certain traditions.

Enthralled

Counting coups, wearing of eagle feathers or donning the bear belt are sacred rites but may point to individuals who were Siphons and created a tradition as a result of their heroic deeds. The stories of Skinwalkers may be suspect. Frontiersman Davy Crockett was renowned for his connection to bears. Shark teeth were often worn as necklaces to protect the wearers. The old Irish used the Rabbit's foot. The Hound of Ulster was said to transform in battle. So many cultures have tales of shape-shifters. Across the globe legends of those who could harness the feral power and strength of nature persist over the years.

I have never encountered a Siphon myself. According to Bobby, his people knew of them but generations long ago. He said they always wore a talisman or had animal companions. I find the concept fascinating and would ask him often about his opinions on how it all worked. He would just raise his hands to the sky and mumble something about "balance or opposing forces." I don't know if Siphons need to actually have a source to call upon their abilities or if it is a catalyst to retrieve something that lies within. Either way, it would seem that Bobby may have been right all along. If the Gläm are to be opposed by anyone it would seem fitting that it would be Siphons.

COMMOTION

Becker had aimed intently. His shot found its mark in a whoosh of air. He saw the man through his scope, clutching his throat and sliding down the tree beside him. Becker moved to grab the flare guns and gave one to Madson as well. Becker glanced at the laptop and motioned to Madson to look at the screen, the other men were holding positions and had no idea that their team leader was bleeding out. They intended to wait until the gunmen realized something was amiss and moved in on the cabin. Then the two of them would let loose flares to blind the attackers. Both men strapped on vests and grabbed flare guns and shotguns. They moved to the windows to wait.

Meanwhile, Gavin was positioned up in a tree to catch any stragglers. His role in this was to ensure that the attackers took the bait and filtered down toward the cabin. Madson and Becker would be exposed after firing the flare guns and it was crucial that the remaining mercenaries all be in attendance for the flare tactic to work effectively. Currently, all was quiet and stillness prevailed, but quickly that would all change. After a few minutes, he could hear footsteps in the leaf litter, faint and distant, but his heightened senses made them out clearly.

Back in the cabin, Becker noticed movement on his screen and motioned to Madson to be on alert. The second-in-command had gone to check on the group leader after hearing no response or directives. He found his team-leader drenched in blood and expired. The second-in-command raised his wrist to his mouth and told the remaining party members to move in on the cabin.

They slowly filtered down between the trees to the darkened cabin. The only light within was Becker's laptop screen. The group proceeded in a semi-circle and drew to a halt when their newly appointed leader raised a fist in the air to halt. It was in that instant that Becker and Madson each fired off two flares in rapid succession from the windows. The night was set ablaze by the four flares in seconds. Madson and Becker stormed out of the kitchen and front doors, strode right up to the blinded men and began unloading their shotguns at point-blank range. Two shots for each aggressor as discussed. The sound was deafening to Gavin but he held his vantage point. Though the men were well trained they had not planned on a counter-offensive nor multiple targets. Despite their body armor, the concussive force of the blasts sent them to the ground. Madson and Becker methodically drew their side arms and finished each of them with a head shot. It was over in mere moments.

Gavin was focused so intently on the commotion that he hadn't noticed the technician from the van until he was directly below him.

ACCUSATIONS

Oni had leveled his gaze on Nathan. He was not a tall man but he had a severe and intimidating glare. At the moment Nathan was seated and dazed from feeding which only accentuated the feeling of being vulnerable. He squirmed unconsciously in the cushions which brought a satisfied grin to Oni's face.

"You have caused me a bit of trouble as of late." His tone was reserved but menacing. His hands were clasped in front of his waist and he slowly wrung them together as he waited for a response. Nathan struggled to rise from the overstuffed sofa and one of the men with Oni held out a scolding hand in a gesture to remain still. Nathan observed and obliged fearfully.

"I had no idea..." Nathan stammered and again Oni gestured to cease.

"It was not you I was speaking to," Oni retorted with an obvious effort to constrain his rage.

Nathan's body went into a state of autopilot as he felt himself recline further. Leto asserted control and put his host at ease with a calming secretion. Leto began to speak in the ancient tongue when Xavier and his armed attendants burst into the room.

"What exactly is going on here?" Xavier demanded from Oni and his crew.

The room grew quiet and tense. The armed men escorting their Immortal masters eyed each other in anticipation of violence.

Meanwhile, Nathan was practically unconscious on the sofa. Oni looked as though he wanted to explode. Xavier was furious as well. The two Immortals were locked in a stare. Xavier motioned to his men to gather Nathan, as they moved to do so Oni's men blocked their path.

"Tell your men to move." Xavier hissed through clenched teeth.

Oni nodded in acquiescence. He knew he had no right to detain them from their master's wishes. His men parted and allowed Nathan to be removed. They hoisted him up and walked him to the door.

"Get him in a car and send him to my office," Xavier shouted.

"I need to explain," Oni interjected.

"Indeed you do." Xavier was seething and it was evident when he spoke.

Xavier's men returned after handing off Nathan to the doorman and a driver. They swiftly slid back into position on either side of their master.

"I fear you misunderstand my motivations, Brother," Oni

added with a hint of pleading in his voice.

"Regardless of your motivations, you have overstepped. I am calling for Council. Plan to meet with our Brothers at the Forest Hills house." With that, Xavier strode out of the room and out of the club to his waiting car. Oni was quiet and contemplative. He paused, allowing his Brother to exit and then left the club as well. Once in the car and moving his phone vibrated, alerting that a text came in.

-Forest Hills.

-Noon.

CONTROL

The technician from the van stumbled to a stop at the base of the tree below Gavin.

Gavin pounced down upon him without thinking. He pummeled the small man with a flurry of clawed strikes, then tore his shoulder and neck to shreds in an instant. The technician scrambled out from under him fueled by pure adrenaline. Blood gushed from his wounds as he raced, crawling on his hands and knees back to the trail. Gavin realized what was about to occur and dove behind the tree as the screaming man detonated one of the claymores on the trail. The explosion ripped through him, tearing him in half and flinging his body in separate directions. The sound rang out through the night and brought Madson and Becker hurriedly to the scene with their sidearms drawn. Gavin was in a fetal position covered in debris. His ears were ringing and his vision was blurry. The blast was jarring and he was rapidly transitioning back to his normal self. Ten feet away, the ravaged legs of the technician spasmed. His upper torso lay face down in the pine needles on the other side of the trail. He gurgled muffled pleas for help. Madson gathered the courage to walk over to what was left of the man. He turned him over to deliver a merciful final blow. To his surprise, as he did so a Gläm slid from his bloody mangled mouth onto the forest floor.

"We got one!" Madson alerted the others.

The Gläm's eyes opened and closed in a slow pulsing rhythm; it began clicking an awful staccato like a cicada.

"Don't grab it with your bare hands," Becker shouted out a warning as he approached.

Gavin struggled to his feet and followed. Becker began to pull on a glove to retrieve the Gläm. Gavin pushed his way in front of them and seized the gore and slime-covered pupa. Its spinal spikes pierced his palm. He did not hear his cohort's cries of disbelief. His mind instantly flooded, his mouth gaped, his eyes rolled back in his head. He stood stiff as a board in a stupor, his limbs shook uncontrollably.

Gavin's mind flooded, body arched backward and spasmed as if an electrical current was pouring through it. His mind's eye peered through a fathomless deep, leagues of water crushed down in the darkness. Glimpses of light pulsed up through the blackness. Volcanic geysers belched tendrils of smoke and lava from the sea floor. Amidst the swirling scene, an immense shadow gently swayed. The instant Gavin was aware of it he felt overwhelmingly terrified. He couldn't see any features or anything that could be considered a face, more so sensed its gaze upon him, then was yanked upwards and could feel his limbs thrashing against the weight of the water yet saw nothing but darkness. The rush of unimaginable volumes of seawater made his ears want to explode. Gavin's head bobbed helplessly against the momentum, then breached the surface violently, flung like a rag doll, into a void of ether. Across the surface of the sea, a myriad of savage scenes played out. Humans and creatures were preyed upon by the Gläm. Dinosaurs, mammoths, Roman soldiers, victims spread out over an inconceivable span of time.

Meanwhile, Becker and Madson were at a loss as to how to help their friend. He was obviously undergoing some sort of experience that they were not privy to. Yet time was of the essence as an explosion, gunfire, and flares had disrupted the still of night. The Gläm's uppermost spike was protruding from the back of Gavin's palm. Becker's instincts told him that the creature was the cause of the problem but didn't know if he should remove it. The last thing he wanted was to cause any further harm. Tearing out the Gläm's barbed quill would shred his hand. Becker grabbed his Leatherman from his hip sheath and motioned for Madson to hold Gavin's arm still. They mouthed the count of three and Becker snapped off the spike with the pliers. The Gläm fell to the ground and Madson caught Gavin and eased him down.

Gavin was out cold.

Madson ripped off his coat and crumpled it up under Gavin's head. Becker had ripped open a med pack from his pouch and proceeded to clean and dress the wound. They were both flying on adrenaline and instinct.

Both men stopped suddenly. A faint buzzing sound was

distracting them. It was coming from the lower half of the technician. The two quickly exchanged a dejected look. Becker shrugged and nodded toward his hands as they were wrapping Gavin's hand. Madson sullenly tromped over to the dead man's legs and began the gruesome task of fishing his cell out from his cargo pockets.

"Text," He shouted to his partner.

"What's it say?" Becker asked, finishing up and securing the bandaging.

-Venue change
-Deliver to Forest Hills
-56 Rowe

CONUNDRUM

Xavier was out of the car before it even came to a stop and strode across the concrete floor of the parking garage to the elevator where Allura was waiting. He was visibly agitated.

Allura said nothing; she simply pushed the button for their floor and remained silent. The doors slid closed and the elevator jostled into motion and began to rise. Xavier impatiently tapped his foot. His hands were clenched into fists on his hips. His eyes were glued on the doors like a bull ready to charge out of the chute. Allura kept quiet and rested her gaze on the bank of buttons in front of her. The cabin came to a stop and he tore down the hallway to his office. Allura followed swiftly behind him. He held the door of his office for her and slammed it shut once she was inside. Nathan was sprawled out on the settee, still unresponsive. Xavier threw himself into his chair and kicked his feet up onto his desk. He rubbed his hands over his eyes in an up-and-down motion.

"I just can't figure out what the hell he's up to?" Xavier

blurted out from behind his hands. He rested his hands on the back of his head and stared at the ceiling, swiveling side to side, in his office chair, in an agitated and fidgety type of motion. Behavior such as this was out of the ordinary for Xavier. The extent of his customary demeanor was known by Allura better than anyone.

Allura shifted to sit across from him. She sensed that his fury was dissipating and thought it may be safe to engage. "You have known Oni for longer than most mortals have lived."

"Yes." Xavier was exasperated but attentive.

"His behavior, as of late, is unlike any you have ever seen before?"

"He has transgressed so severely," Xavier paused, puzzled, "and he normally would be the first to defend our ways."

"From what I know of Oni, he seems like a clever man."

Xavier nodded in agreement. "He calculates every angle."

Allura noted his reaction and continued. "So, if his behavior is abnormal and you do not think he has gone mad, then what remains?"

Xavier sat up in his chair. Allura sat stock still with her legs crossed and hands folded on her knee. She was alert and composed as always, waiting quietly for Xavier to put things together.

"He has an agenda. He would never act in such a way without cause."

Allura remained quiet. She listened patiently, and waited for the pieces to fall into place.

Xavier jumped to his feet, thunderstruck. His eyes were round as saucers.

Enthralled

"Whatever he is planning is huge if he would risk so much," Xavier exclaimed and flopped back into his chair.

CLEAN UP

Becker was starting to get frazzled. Gavin was unconscious on the ground. There were claymores to deactivate and remove. Additionally, a pile of bodies and weapons needed to be dealt with. Luckily, the location was remote and the commotion hadn't drawn any attention.

Yet.

Not to mention Madson was now covered in gore up to his elbows and staring dazedly at the cell phone he had retrieved. True to his form, Becker had anticipated just such a contingency. Knowing the unpredictable nature of his situation he had coordinated with a colleague from his life before the police force.

Few people impressed Becker with their preparedness, yet this Cleaner was always held in high esteem by him and knew that calling in W, as the cleaner was known by, would yield the best result on any occasion. Becker texted, "*clean up*" and almost instantly the response came back "*45.*" He had arranged with W in advance as a precaution and now felt considerably relieved that he was on route, although it did not entirely diminish the tasks at hand.

Enthralled

"Hey!" Becker shouted to Madson, snapping him out of his daze. "We need to get the van off the road, gotta find the keys."

A forlorn look spread across Madson's face as he began to rummage through the pockets of the lower half of the technician. Madson searched to no avail. Becker was up and moving to disarm the mines. Madson saw him moving with his flashlight into the tree line and resigned himself to search the other bodies. It took close to half an hour to remove the claymores and stow them safely back into their cases.

When Becker returned from the woods, Madson was still ransacking the multitude of pockets on their deceased adversaries when Becker tossed him the car keys.

"Leader usually drives," Becker chuckled at Madson's expense.

Madson mumbled a string of curses under his breath as he started to walk down the drive toward the van. As he did, a pair of headlights turned into the drive. His hand flew to his holster. "That's my guy," Becker shouted. "He's early."

A second set of headlights followed as the two vehicles approached, both men waited tensely. An all-black tinted-out Denali rolled to a stop. The driver-side window rolled down. Becker dug into his pocket and produced a large gold coin. He walked over and handed it through the window.

"Your coin and whatever gear we don't need." Becker motioned to the pile of mercenaries.

"Fantastic," W said as he swung open the door. Simultaneously the rear passenger door swung open and one of his assistants sprang

90

into action. He immediately began stripping gear from the bodies of the hired killers. The second assistant popped out of the pest control van. W noticed the exasperated look on Madson's face and his bloody hands and forearms.

"Above the visor," he chuckled. "They always have two sets."

Madson began grumbling profanities again as he moved to the kitchen to wash up.

W walked over to Becker. W towered over him. He was a tall rectangular man, slim with neatly cropped auburn beard and hair.

"How many?"

"Six and a mountain lion," Becker smirked, shrugging. "Long story."

"I count seven," W added flatly without ever even looking around.

"Oh, he's not dead," Becker quickly interjected. "He's knocked out, but with us."

W just smirked and walked away. "Long story right?"

COMATOSE

Nathan was still out cold, mostly due to Leto exerting some efforts to keep him that way. Leto quietly listened as Allura and Xavier discussed the situation. Throughout the conversation, he had been listening and processing the encounter with Oni at the club. Leto was thankful that he had at least been able to finish his meal before the unpleasant interchange. It is difficult for a Gläm to focus with an empty belly. That thought struck him with an epiphany. Things fell in place like cascading dominoes. He dared to break his silent observation.

Sir? Leto spoke telepathically to Xavier.

"*You've decided to join us?*" Xavier responded, " *I was wondering when you'd chime in.*"

Leto was more than nervous, he was scared. He was afraid of what his insinuations might set in motion. His distracted demeanor was loosening his hold over Nathan's comatose state. Yet he had to speak.

Sir, I may have some insights pertaining to the Oni situation. Leto paused momentarily, *If I may share?*

"Of course," Xavier quickly encouraged. "But out loud so we all can hear." Xavier spoke the direction to the room, to alert Allura of the coming discourse. She perked up and listened intently.

An idea struck me while listening to both of you. Yet I need to talk through it to determine how accurate it may be.

"Proceed," Xavier nudged impatiently. Allura readied her pen and pad.

Yes, Sir, Leto gathered his courage as Nathan began to stir. *My first observation is in regard to the veil Oni employed. He was somehow able to cloud my hosts' minds and my own mind and memories. I am only able to do so with those I am feeding on or connected to. He was also able to obscure the events from his Immortal brethren. Has any of our kind been able to do so previously?*

Xavier thought hard on it, scratching his chin as Allura feverishly scribbled notes. "Not to my knowledge," he concluded.

Leto began again. *That ability is new then. We have established Oni's adherence to our ways and his calculating manner. So, for him to behave erratically and out of accord with age-old standards would be incredibly out of character. These actions would be of great risk to himself and to what he has built over the years. It is my opinion that given his track record, he would only risk so much if the reward was worth it.*

"Yes, yes," Xavier interjected. "We've established that. What's the reward? What is he after?"

Leto paused, the last thing he wanted was to offend his master. He had seen the results of his fury. *Sir, we have already experienced a portion of the reward he sought. His ability to veil us all so resolutely is proof. The question that begs answering is how he acquired his new found powers. That's what struck me after feeding. He got them by feeding. Therefore if he has developed something new and different, it must be because he has a new food source.*

"Impossible." Xavier was confounded. "There is nothing new to be had!"

Sir, there is the product of his transgression. My host's brother is a Siphon. My theory is that Oni has been feeding on Siphons. Even worse is the fact that he has been creating them to do so.

The room fell quiet. Allura's pen went still. Xavier sat motionless, and stared blankly. Nathan sat up rubbing his eyes and face like a toddler rising from an afternoon nap. He gazed around the room confused. Xavier spoke softly as if he was recalling from a distant place and time.

"How long has this been going on?"

I have no idea, Sir. But it does explain something else.

"What?" Xavier's reply was quiet, his face still aghast.

The crash that killed Mrs. Cross.

ANTIQUUS LIBELLUS
SERVATOR JOHN THOMAS

On Immortal Physiology

It is difficult to know the actual makeup of an Immortal. To my knowledge, no Servator has ever actually destroyed one. Even capturing one has eluded us. So no real studies or observations have been conducted. One thing I do know is they are tough as hell to kill. They have the ability to regenerate damaged tissue at an alarming rate. This ability also applies to broken bones, burns, and severe trauma. At this point, bridging the gap between legends and reality seems fitting. Vampiric tales talk of killing via a stake through the heart and decapitation. These methods would also be suited for Gläm. The stake would most likely be used for the Gläm itself during its pupa phase. While the separation of the head from the body would seem best for an Immortal. I have heard accounts of them being burned, shot, and crushed to no avail. They have evolved to live up to their names.

Gläm, while in a first-stage host, would be the easiest to eradicate. Unfortunately at the cost of the human ward. The Gläm are quite tough in their own right as they are armored and rather spiky. The most vulnerable of their kind

Enthralled

are those that haven't been implanted in a host and are awaiting transfer. If we were ever able to find and demolish one of their holding locations it could serve a crippling blow. They are also vulnerable while feeding, but again, the cost is the host and often the Peeler. Immortals still need to feed especially if they have suffered any injuries. They need the proteins to rebuild. The way in which Immortals feed is also a mystery but again going back to vampire lore it is a more direct method than a Gläm and host.

The Immortals have a Glämour that can subdue victims through a combination of pheromones and bioluminescence.

Even removing the head is questionable. As they are born through asexual budding. It is not known if like the hydra it would simply split off and regrow. Yet, having personally seen Gläm pupae die, their fragile nature when plucked out belies that life out of water has changed them. So my gut tells me that beheading an Immortal would be the best bet.

COINAGE

W walked over to the back of the Denali. Becker watched as he counted out body bags. W flipped a latch just above the bumper. A ramp sprung out, which he pulled out and lowered to the ground. The ramp latched in place once it was fully extended. One of his assistants took the body bags and walked back over to the mercenaries. W then guided a gurney down the ramp, which seemed to be modified for all-terrain use. He pushed the gurney over to where his assistant had begun working and walked back over to Becker.

"I never thought you'd part with that double eagle," he spoke quietly, almost to himself.

"Desperate times call for desperate measures," Becker responded.

"What have you gotten yourself into with all of this?" W waved his hand in a subtle gesture.

"You wouldn't believe me if I told you," Becker chuckled.

"I've done a lot of cleanups and seen a lot of different things, but I never seen whatever those things are."

Becker was astounded. He was not aware of W ever even being near the Gläm, but somehow he had noticed.

"It might be better if you just forgot you ever saw it. Those things are at the center of whatever the hell is going on here. I never intended to get mixed up in all this, but now I'm in it." Becker sighed, "It doesn't mean that you have to be in it as well."

"Do you want me to dispose of it?" W asked flatly.

"I hadn't even thought of that, we've been bagging them to examine. Things have gotten rather escalated as of late. It might be better if you let me deal with it."

Becker noticed a wry look on W's face and sensed where this was headed.

W smirked and began, "Do you know why I asked for the double eagle? It is because it's unique. Yes, it has monetary value but there are very few like it. Whatever that thing is, I've never seen one before." W paused and looked directly at Becker. "So, I want it."

Becker quickly interjected, "That would be getting you involved in a whole lot of craziness. I just don't think it's worth it."

"How about this? What if I take it for examination and share the results with you? Would that be helpful?"

Becker thought for a moment. Honestly, it would be very helpful and he knew that W was incredibly skilled and intelligent. He also knew that his discretion was superb.

"Yes, it would be helpful, but you must understand that the risk is also great."

W chuckled, "In my line of work the risk is always great."

Gavin had started to stir. His head was throbbing. His ears were ringing. He sat himself upright, startling one of W's assistants who most likely presumed him dead. Gavin rubbed his eyes and realized that his hand had been bandaged.

The dead Gläm was still on the ground next to him, its severed barb laying next to it.

Gavin surveyed the scene wondering where these new people had come from. Seeing his confusion, Madson sauntered over to help him up.

"Doing okay?" He asked.

Gavin couldn't really figure out how to respond and half-heartedly nodded with a groan. Words were difficult at the moment but he was compelled to keep the spike that was pulled from his hand. He was unable to express this to Madson so he pointed to it with his uninjured hand. Madson looked down at the dead Gläm

"Yah… that guy took you on some sort of wild ride."

He was trying to gently guide Gavin over toward Becker. Gavin grunted while planting his feet and vigorously pointed more closely to the barb. Madson was still stumped. Gavin now began pointing to his injured hand and the spike. Madson was catching on now. He reached down and used the van keys like a spatula to scoop it up and place it in Gavin's bandaged palm. Gavin grumbled an affirmation and allowed himself to be led over to Becker and W by Madson.

"What's the plan?" Madson interjected as he approached

assisting Gavin.

Madson had his arm wrapped around Gavin trying to prop him up. Gavin was still a bit wobbly. Becker and W had been speaking privately, figuring out an agreement of sorts.

Becker thought for a moment and asked W, "Can you and your team finish up at the cabin?"

W nodded. The small gesture was enough to assure Becker that everything would be handled properly. Madson could sense the wheels turning behind Becker's eyes, a plan was being set into motion.

Becker shouted to W's assistants, "Grab three of the flak jackets!"

"Then pull the vehicles out behind the cabin," Becker waved, pointing to where he wanted them parked. He turned to Madson, "And let's start piling gear into the extermination van."

Becker shook hands with W. "I'll be in touch," he said, bidding farewell with a nod.

W smiled, "Hope so."

The trio hopped in the van and headed to Forest Hills. Madson jumped into the driver's seat. Becker did not ride shotgun; he immediately got his laptop out and onto his lap in one of the bench seats along the sides of the van. There was a single seat mounted in the rear of the van into the door which swung outwards and Gavin sat there. Their departure was unceremonious at best and they did not interact much until they got out to the main roads. Becker was busy trying to get some images of the location to have a better idea as to how to handle the whole situation. It seemed as though the area in question was dotted with gated communities and rather lavish homes. Becker found the address and was able to begin formulating a plan.

Once they got out on the interstate Madson gruffly broke the silence, "You guys are killing me, somebody's going to have to tell me what the hell happened back there."

Becker and Gavin both chuckled.

"Which part?" Becker inquired

"All of it!" Madson blurted out.

"The part where we killed the bad guys?"

"No," Madson snapped. "That part I get!"

"Then which part?"

"How about the part where Gavin became the cat-man or how about the part where he disappeared into some weird trance?" Madson huffed in exasperation waiting for a response.

Becker chuckled, then looked back at Gavin and added, "Well, I don't really know how to explain it, maybe we should ask the man himself?"

Gavin clammed up real quick. He had been trying to figure out a way to make the spike from the Gläm into another talisman. He had found some zip ties and electrical tape and was trying to make a hoop for the spike. Becker noticed that he was fidgeting with something.

"How's your hand doing?"

Gavin sheepishly looked up at Becker who was now craned intently looking at him. Gavin did not speak, he simply began to unravel the bandages from his hand. The bandages had a considerable amount of dried blood on them yet when he removed them there were no lacerations on his hand. Becker was flabbergasted.whistling in disbelief. Madson was trying to see what was going on in the rearview mirror.

"What is it? What's going on?"

Gavin shrugged his shoulders, "I don't know, one minute the cuts were there and now they're just not."

"How is that possible?" Madson asked from the driver's seat.

"Do you think you're ready to talk about what happened? When the spike was in your hand?" Becker had adopted a pleading tone.

"Sure, I guess. It's all kind of crazy; you guys are going to think I'm nuts."

"I literally watched you turn into a cat and jump clear up into a tree," Madson interjected. "I think we went past crazy a while ago!"

"If you can try to remember," Becker paused, "Start at the beginning."

"Well, for some reason I just felt like I had to grab it."

Becker held up his hand for Gavin to stop for a second.

"Do you care if I take notes, Gavin? I feel like this is very important. We should document it."

"No, that's fine."

Becker wiggled around in his seat and got ready to type.

Gavin began again. "I felt like I had to grab it, not sure why, but when I did all of a sudden it was like I was being sucked down into the ocean. Real deep, I could feel it pressing down on me and there was a presence or a feeling that there was somebody there. Only there really wasn't anybody there, just this giant sort of thing. It was like a giant pillar of living stuff, kind of hard to really pinpoint but it was in my head, not talking to me but there and once it realized that I knew it was there it cast me out. It pushed me away. The next thing I knew I was flying upwards out of the ocean I could feel all the water rushing past me and then I saw all these horrible scenes of violence and death and destruction. The scenes spread out from the beginning of time, all different people and creatures, all getting torn up and it kind of just kept going on until nowadays. I don't really know how to explain it, but first I was wrapped up in where these things came from and then shoved away."

Becker stopped typing, waited a moment deep in thought, and asked, "Could you get any sort of location, Anything that would point to where it actually was?"

"No, not really it just was deep down in the water, it was dark, real dark. This thing was just sort of swaying there, it was kind of like it was everywhere all around me but it was also right there too. Sorry, I know that that doesn't help much."

"No, that's okay.This actually tells us a lot," Becker said soothingly.

"Still doesn't make things any more clear for me," Madson added, rubbing his head.

"How do you think it is that your hand healed completely?" Becker inquired.

"Oh, I don't really know, like I said it just kind of was there

103

and then it was fixed."

"I have a theory on it," Becker mused. "I think that somehow, just like the mountain lion, you were able to tap into the Gläm ability and not only did it initiate the vision you had, but it also allowed you to heal. The part I don't get is how you were able to heal after you were disconnected."

"I really don't know," Gavin replied, looking down at the bandages on the floor of the van.

"Well, of course I'm glad you're all mended up," Becker spoke reassuringly. "But it is definitely intriguing and it makes me wonder just how this whole thing works."

Gavin grew quiet and went back to fidgeting around with the spike pendant he was trying to make. Madson had no further input, all of this was very far out of his wheelhouse. Becker went back to typing. For a time the three of them went back to a quiet and introspective car ride down to the city.

ANTIQUUS LIBELLUS SERVATOR NILES BECKER

After witnessing Gavin's remarkable regenerative and transformative abilities, something dawned on me. This will be my first entry in the Old Book, but I have surmised that it may be necessary given what has been transpiring as of late. When I was a kid at the Academy in New England, I spent a large chunk of time preoccupied with Lovecraft's tales, and it would seem that there have been no connections made to the Fomore. The Fomore are rooted deep in Celtic legend, and although it may be speculative at best, it may add up as to why they are absent from any of the Servators' notes. From what I have read, many of the books were destroyed in Alexandria. Given the occupation of the Emerald Isles by the Romans and the Christians, it would add up that any of the Irish contributors' books may have been destroyed when the great libraries were burned.

The Fomore were said to have come from the deep; some have said that they came from an underworld, but mostly they are regarded as beings that came from the deep sea. That may have meant that they existed in grottos beneath the waves or cave systems. They were purportedly deformed. Some were even gigantic; the Fomor clashed with early inhabitants of the Hibernians to capture their lands.

Enthralled

Moreso their abilities, intentions, and origins definitely match with the Gläm but what is even more intriguing is their progeny and god. It was said that a pact or treaty was made between the Tuatha de Dannan and the Fomorians. Tales told of the offspring of the Fomori and the inhabitants having astounding abilities. The story of King Bres, being one of the crossbreeds, suggests Gläm involvement. It would seem that this Bres was a ruthless and cruel king to the Tuatha de Dannan and favored his Fomorian kin. He had a hypnotic air about him and was dazzling to behold. It was also said that the god and origin of the Fomor was the Great Worm. This not only connects with what Gavin reported witnessing but also with his newfound abilities. It may also be incredibly important to know that the Glämhave a singular place of origin and possibly even discover the location of it. It may mean they could be destroyed in one fell swoop.

WRAP UP

W's crew worked tirelessly until dawn crept up behind the mountains. W took exceeding pride in his attention to detail. It may seem an odd concept that customer service and word-of-mouth would be essential in such a clandestine service industry, yet it was essential to his operation. Every drop of blood was sprayed with a chemical solution and covered with leaf litter. Each shell casing was gathered and every bullet hole addressed. He double-checked that the doors of the cabin were locked as well as the vehicles left behind. Once he was certain that everything was left in an inconspicuous and tidy manner, he gathered his crew and left for his home.

Stony Creek was a little over a half hour away. W's funeral home looked like something from a medieval tale. It was made of stout blocks of stone in an era when craftsmanship meant something. He found the place, when he retired from government work, in a state of disrepair. He invested in remodeling and repairing and spared no expense in doing so. The place was a fortress, monitored by cameras and motion sensors. As the Denali glided into the driveway and pulled around back, the garage door opened. Rolling carts were situated against the wall. His assistants exited the vehicle and began loading the body bags onto the carts. A gated lift lowered down beneath the floor of the garage where a service tunnel led directly to the embalming room and incinerator. It took two carts to move the bodies into the area. His two workers began loading bodies into the incinerator while collecting weapons and gear into large black duffel bags for W to examine.

"Please put the duffels in my office when you are done."

W had an office just off of the embalming room. At first glance, it seemed typical. Bookshelves lined the walls, a modern but spartan desk in the far corner, and a drafting table with an adjustable overhead light in the opposite corner. W proceeded to the center shelf on the wall. He slid a small bust of Alexander the Great to one side, revealing a latch. The shelf shifted toward him and slid to his left revealing a rough-hewn passage and set of stairs heading down. Remnants of the Underground Railroad provided him with this most private retreat. He approached a darkened open area and, with a word, lights illuminated the darkness. A cavern of stone large enough to park five or six vehicles revealed itself. A Persian carpet covered the floor and a large ebony wood table sat in the center of the space. Along the curved walls, ornate shelves rose up to the domed ceiling. LED lights lit each set of shelves. W moved to a shelf with a glass cylinder filled with embalming fluid. He gently slid the body of the Gläm inside and placed the cap back on it. Beside the cylinder was a fossil, one of the rarest on the planet. It was about the size of a pizza box and held upright at a 45-degree angle by a sturdy metal tripod. There in bas-relief was another Gläm trapped in stone.

RESTLESS

Xavier didn't rest, never really slept actually. His mind was a blur of possibilities. The Immortals were set to meet at the Forest Hills house later that day. Xavier had paced his office for hours in the darkness and now the sun was rising. Immortals never needed to sleep but sometimes Xavier would recline and drift toward the Source. The practice was relaxing and felt rejuvenating to connect. No such respite was to be had, concerns over Oni's motives had him perplexed and perturbed simultaneously. He couldn't fathom why Oni would deviate from the ways they had sworn to uphold. It was also vexing that Oni had been able to hide all of this from the hive mind all Gläm shared. If Leto had been even remotely accurate with his musings, it meant that Oni had indeed found a way to surpass his brethren.

Dawn had broken across the rooftops of Manhattan. Xavier needed to prepare for the Council of Immortals both physically and mentally. He had not survived and risen to power by being unprepared. Yet at this moment, he had no idea what to expect, especially because he would never have anticipated this sort of behavior from one of his own. He reached for his phone and pondered for a moment, hesitated to text Allura but after an elongated sigh sent the message:

-Please come to my office.

He knew that she would be awake. That wasn't the issue. He needed her counsel. More so than ever he was concerned that her secret would be revealed. He had sworn to her that he would do everything in his power to keep it hidden. Now more than ever the risk of her undisclosed past threatened to come to light.

A knock came at the door. Quietly and gracefully Allura glided in and closed the door behind her.

"How can I be of service?" Allura dutifully inquired.

Xavier strode across the room and hugged her close to him. His embrace was nearly crushing the wind from her. He whispered to her, "Daughter, I am so worried."

EXCURSION

The exterminator van crossed the RFK bridge toward Queens as the sun was rising. The trio decided to have Madson drive. Becker needed to check equipment and Gavin was still trying to get his head straight. Becker was wearing one of the jackets from the mercenaries and had two more for Madson and Gavin, although Madson's may not fit so well. The plan was to locate the place in Forest Hills and then grab some food and wait.

They were able to find the Gläms facility in Forest Hills from the address off of the technician's phone. It was gated and looked very much like many of the other homes in the area. The home was grand and had a rather European aesthetic. There were three floors and a tiled roof, and was stoutly made of brick. The driveway led through a portico to a three-car garage and an ample cobbled parking area. There was what appeared to be a guard house built into the portico wall for vehicles entering. Not too much else could be gathered from the distance they were surveilling from. They also did not want to draw attention to themselves at that early hour of the morning. The general layout would have to be enough. So now the objective was to grab some food.

Becker knew a spot. It was called the Neptune Diner and it served food 24 hours a day. The name made Becker chuckle as they exited the vehicle and approached. It struck him as both fitting and funny given the nature of their adversaries. The diner also sported a tiled roof and a parking area around the back. The diner had stucco walls and rocked a '70s vibe.

The three men bellied up to the counter. Madson immediately asked for coffee for the three of them. The middle-aged woman behind the counter nodded an affirmation and produced three cups from under the counter. The coffee tasted like it was made the day before and none of them cared one bit; it was glorious.

They ordered before she even had a chance to hand out menus. Gavin asked for pancakes, Becker and Madson got eggs over easy and bacon with rye toast. Becker started explaining their approach. The food came quickly. He began laying out the steps between bites.

"First we buzz in at the gate around nine." Becker stacked a bite of toast with bacon and crunched heartily.

"Once the vehicle's parked," he swallowed a gulp of coffee, "we gear up and then try to gain access to the garage."

Madson and Gavin nodded in understanding while chomping.

"From the garage we would need to find a way to the basement. Once there, beneath the Immortals we plant the remaining Claymores below them. The hope is to bring them crashing into the

113

basement and dispatch them amid the chaos. Just like last time."

"Just like last time," Madson agreed.

Taking a sip of his coffee, Gavin held his reservations. Would it really be that simple, or, as the old detectives put it, "Just like last time?"

They had polished off their breakfast and had a general plan figured out. The waitress took their plates and asked if they wanted more coffee. All three asked for more.

Madson asked, "Is there any pie?"

Gavin and Becker got a laugh from that. Madson got a slice of warm apple pie and scraped his plate clean with his fork. They settled up the bill and headed back to the van. Becker hopped behind the wheel and drove back to the Forest Hills mansion.

Only a few minutes before nine, Becker buzzed at the gate and announced, "Pest Erase." The gates opened and he slowly drove toward the portico.

CONVENTION

Xavier and Allura had arrived at the Forest Hills house before sunrise. The rest of the Immortals were not due to arrive for hours. Xavier had brought a security detail to sweep the house prior to the gathering. His team had swept the house and grounds quickly and efficiently. They had completed the task and were preparing the main hall for the Council. The space usually served as a banquet hall. An oak table occupied the center of the room, regally carved chairs were placed around it. One taller and more ornate chair was positioned at each end of the table. At the head with his back to the windows would be Xavier and at the opposite end, Oni. Allura was delicately and diligently writing and putting out place cards. Xavier wanted everything to be just to his liking, especially in tense meetings such as this one.

Allura had also been given very explicit directions on how to handle Gavin and his colleagues. The van and cell phones were tracked via Allura's cell phone. The team's demise was known to Xavier. The moment the technician and his ward were killed, the rest of the Gläm were aware. To his chagrin, Xavier was forced to admit he was relieved the mission had failed. Given the recent developments, Oni's machinations combined with Leto's suspicions, it may be more advantageous to them that Gavin was alive. He wanted him to remain so and vehemently expressed this to Allura.

So, when they arrived at the Forest Hills house, Allura was prepared. Fortunately, she had just finished the place cards for the Immortals. When the exterminator van buzzed in she quickly moved to the portico guard house to receive them. Allura composed herself, tossing her braid over her shoulder and adjusting her blazer once inside. An aluminum clipboard sat at the desk which had been rigged in advance. When the van reached the sliding window she greeted Becker.

"Good morning!" Allura greeted them effervescently.

Becker smiled amicably, then shot Madson and Gavin a look that said, *Too easy*, as Allura handed him the clipboard to sign in.

As Allura passed the clipboard to him, she pulled the pin from the pressurized cartridge inside of it, hastily sliding the service window shut.

Fumes jetted from the end of the metal case.

Becker's eyes grew wide as the greenish-yellow gas cloud filled the interior and then they closed shut just as quickly. Before he could utter an exclamation of warning to the others to hold their breath, he was slumped forward against the steering wheel. Within seconds all three men were unconscious.

Allura waited for a minute, to ensure the the effects of the gas had taken hold. She watched her phone's timer anxiously. Given the time crunch, 60 seconds seemed like forever. Allura then pressed the intercom button to signal she needed assistance.

"Portico," was all she said, as a precaution against prying ears.

Two men in face masks sprang from the garage. Allura got into the driver's seat as the occupants' wrists were being zip-tied together. The guards put the three of them on the floor of the van. They slid the panel door shut and banged three times on the door. Allura put the van in drive and headed toward Club Decadence.

DOMINATION

Allura was confident that she had not been seen by any of the Immortals. They were not set to arrive for a few hours. She needed to get the van back to the club in Manhattan and then return to the meeting. She would have to hope that her instructions would be followed by the guards at the club. The trip was close to an hour; she would need to execute a quick turnaround in order to be back and get composed as the guests arrived. She pulled into the loading dock and two men were waiting as per the plan. She exited the van, tossed the keys to one of them and climbed into the back seat of an idling black sedan. The driver immediately pulled away to return her whence she came. If traffic permitted, she could be there with an hour to spare.Allura was worried about Xavier, having never seen him act like this before,and was worried about whether her presence was making it worse. Her own secrets threatened to be laid bare and they could be damaging for Xavier given the circumstances.

The sedan glided in toward the gate. She did not want to

announce herself as a precautionary measure. The driver said simply, "Xavier," without being aware it was Allura who mentally suggested he do so. Her power of suggestion was powerful and yet subtle. Her gifts had always gone unnoticed. Perhaps this was the reason Xavier insisted she accompany him for this event despite her being a Siphon herself. They passed through the portico and parked in the garage. Allura hurried toward the banquet hall to stand beside Xavier and receive their guests. She smoothed her skirt and straightened her collar.

"Everything went smoothly I presume?" Xavier inquired with barely a whisper.

"So far, Sir," she quietly replied.

The gate buzzer sounded and announced O'Balor and his entourage. The Irishman was notorious for showing up early and staying late. He and his crew greeted Xavier and Allura warmly. They chatted a moment before the gate buzzed again.

Nathan had arrived.

Xavier's countenance wrinkled as he was supposed to be there with Allura to greet their guests. Nathan joined them and slid into the conversation casually but did not escape the glare of Xavier. Once O'Balor and his cohorts were seated, Xavier scolded Nathan privately.

"Punctuality," he growled.

"My apologies," Nathan bowed his head in remorse, "I'm still running the accounting firm by day, Sir."

"Nonetheless, these are important matters."

The remaining Immortals arrived in waves. Next was Volk,

who was even taller than Xavier and practically had to duck upon entering. Malvito and Brujo showed up simultaneously. Jiangshi followed soon after. Last to arrive was Oni, just a few minutes before noon.

Everyone was shown to their seats and a beverage cart circled the table. Each Immortal sat at the table and their attendants were seated behind them in the chairs placed around the perimeter of the room.

Oni sat at the end of the table near the entrance. Xavier took his place at the far end of the table across from him. In accordance with the ways of the Old One's, Xavier would speak first as he called the Council together. Once everyone was settled and comfortable he rapped his big bony knuckles three times slowly on the table to commence.

"My brothers, I will not waste your time," Xavier announced. "I have called you here because one of our brothers has broken with the Old Ways and I ask him now to explain himself before all of you."

There was a moment of darting eyes and sideways glances but Oni rose to his feet to speak.

"My brothers, I have grown tired of being patient. I have parted from the Old Ways." He paused and leaned forward with both palms pressed on the table. His eyes scanned the faces of each of his brothers.

"I have transgressed. Yet my mistake may be one of the greatest discoveries for our advancement in centuries. Perhaps, in all time."

ANTIQUUS LIBELLUS
SERVATOR BOBBY HAYES

Rosie

Suffering writhes around the Gläm. Their existence is sustained on the pain and misery of humanity. I must admit that it would seem that tragedy sets a Servator on the path to serve. Those tragedies were more often than not a result of the Gläms' involvement.

My own call to action was also such a case. Now as I prepare to walk off into twilight I felt I should share this part of my story. I share this to let whomever is committed to walk this road find solace in a story. A story of my one and only love Rosie May. As it is the practice to rewrite the book passed to you, our story will live on. Her memory will endure as my love for her always will. It was her loss that led me to this way of life.

Rosie was the kindest person I've ever met. She went out of her way to treat others well. She grew up feeling left out and didn't want anyone to feel that way. Her dad was a black jazz musician and her mom was Shawnee. She grew up tagging along on the music scene and never really set any roots down. Her father Reggie was a victim of the Gläm. He had taken a deal to rise up in the music

Enthralled

world. The tragic part was although he was successful, he fathered Rosie, while under their control. Rosie never knew any of this, I was able to put the pieces together when I became a Servator. Her mother Daisy was also unaware but was nevertheless a casualty of the Gläm. We met at Cafe Lena in the Sixties and spent every moment together. We went to Woodstock and that was where she was abducted by the Gläm. She was set up on a blanket with a cardboard sign offering Tarot and Palm readings. That was her gift. It was also how they found her.

When they took her from me I swore to do whatever I could to stop them.

DEVELOPMENT

Oni let his statement hang in the air. He wanted the notion to gestate in his brothers' mind for a moment. He began to slowly circle the table while speaking.

"As we all are aware, it has been our duty for millennia to eradicate any Siphon." He paused after the statement and delivered an icy glare at Allura. His action did not go unnoticed by Xavier.

"It was my duty to exterminate them rather often due to the prowess inherited from my hosts. My discovery was a result of one such mission during the Woodstock music festival. It had come to our attention that a certain young woman named Rosie was in attendance and the event would provide the opportunity to address the problem. The place was a madhouse. Finding her there seemed hopeless. On the contrary, when we arrived on the scene amidst a sea of attendees walking for what felt like an eternity, there she was. It was almost like she had been beckoning us. She offered to read my palm which I indulged. When she began, I reeled as I immediately felt her presence in my mind. She also was aghast as she began. She fainted. We scooped her up in her own blanket and whisked her away. As I carried her, I could not control the urge to feed. It was inevitable. So, when we were secluded I succumbed to my hunger. It was then that I became concerned that she had been using drugs as my mind began to whirl. Everyone around us was on something. It would make sense. Yet it was not the case. I left her there, wrapped in a blanket in the woods. She passed after I fed.

"I rejoined our team and made the long trek home. As we walked, I felt as though my thoughts were invaded by those around me but shook it off. Over the next few days I realized that whatever talent she possessed had manifested within me."

Oni had circled the entirety of the table and now sat back into his seat. He paused to gauge the reactions of his brethren. All were in silent awe, except for Xavier who was glaring down the table at him.

"What does any of that have to do with the Cross woman?"

Xavier had to be careful to not make an outright accusation given the protocols of Council. He was furious but needed to keep his composure.

Oni smiled and replied, "Isn't it obvious?"

Xavier waved his hand in an upward motion. "Illuminate us."

"I developed enhanced abilities by consuming a Siphon. I grow tired of being patient. If we grow more powerful it will accelerate us achieving our goals."

"So you knowingly created a Siphon," Xavier rose in outrage, "just to eat it?"

Oni's crocodile grin returned. "Not just one," Oni moved his hand in a circular motion indicating those at the table. "There wouldn't be enough to go around."

"What you're suggesting is cannibalism."

Oni stood up in defiance and responded. "Hardly. What I'm suggesting is progress."

CONTAINED

Gavin was the first to start to stir. They had been transferred to a room but it was too dark to make much out. He could feel that he was on a sofa of some sort. The room was damp and cool, that much he could tell. His hands were zip tied in front of him. Madson was beside him on the couch, out cold, but he wasn't sure where Becker was.

Gavin began wriggling toward Madson. He gently tried to nudge his friend awake with his bound hands, careful not to make too much noise and draw unwanted attention. Madson's head just lolled back to its original position. Yet there was a low hum of a motor running in the room, perhaps air conditioning, so he decided to try.

"Becker," he whispered hoarsely. "Hey, Beck." There was an urgency in his voice yet still no response. He struggled to stand up, the sofa was deeply cushioned and his whole body was wobbly. Gavin scooched his hips toward the edge of the sofa in an effort to get his feet beneath him, and in doing so he felt the mountain lion claw bounce against his chest. Immediately he was worried about using it given his condition and circumstances. It would most definitely help, though, what with his restraints and the lighting. He was torn as to whether he could remain in control, the last thing he wanted to do was harm his friends.

* * *

Xavier was nonplussed at Oni's casual and condescending retort. He couldn't imagine his brethren would be agreeable to breeding Siphons like cattle for consumption. Yet when he surveyed those seated around the table, he was shocked at how many of those present appeared to be nodding in agreement. He needed to regroup and reassess before things got out of hand. Luckily, he realized, since he called for the meeting he could also end it.

"There is much to think on," he spoke slowly with a cautious tone. "Let us conclude for today and reconvene in two days' time."

None gathered there spoke any more of it and began to leave. The Immortals gathered their entourages and quietly began to exit. Decorum dictated that whomever called for Council was in charge of the proceedings and also established the tone. Xavier made no urgency over departure; he did not want to be perceived as frazzled in any way. If this madness persisted Xavier may need to report to the Baron. Doing so at this point may be regarded as frailty.

Oni was the last to leave, he made no remarks but made sure to pause and give a wry smirk to Allura. Xavier noticed the unkind gesture and was able to contain himself.

As soon as everyone had left, Xavier motioned to his

attendants to leave. The cars were running and waiting in the courtyard. Xavier slid into the backseat and Allura joined him.

"To the Club," he sighed "as quickly as possible."

* * *

Gavin decided it was worth the risk, instinct screamed to get out of there. So, he closed his eyes, took a deep breath, grasped the claw, opened his eyes and could immediately see the surroundings despite the darkness. Quickly Gavin worked at his own bindings, gnawing at them while twisting his wrists. After breaking free, he set about removing his companions' zip ties with a pocket knife, but found it difficult to open the lock blade given his condition. He closed his eyes and exhaled while attempting to relax and revert back; change refused to ensue. Something was inhibiting the transition. It was at that moment the door slowly creaked open behind him.

COLLABORATION

Even though Xavier rushed to get to the club his plan remained the same: keep Gavin from interfering with the meeting and make sure he didn't end up falling into Oni's hands. Xavier could at least take some small satisfaction in the fact that something had gone right today.

His driver pulled up and waited while the car remained running. Xavier was headed back to his office to plan for the upcoming meeting at the club. Allura and Nathan exited the vehicle and were met by four hulking attendants at the entrance. The guards parted and allowed them to pass and lead the way through the club. They stopped in front of a familiar room; it made Nathan chuckle inwardly. *This was Xavier's private room*, he thought, the spot where Nathan's crazy journey had begun.

Allura opened the door slowly to the dark room. She flipped on the overhead lights and was startled to find that Gavin was up and on his feet. When he turned to face her she was even more aghast at his countenance. Gavin looked absolutely feral, his eyes were wild and his face snarled and contorted. He spun and looked as though he was preparing to pounce on whoever entered. Madson and Becker were still unconscious with their hands bound. Gavin began to growl and slink toward Allura. The guards quickly entered and put themselves between Gavin and Allura. He still did not waiver; he continued at a slow and methodical pace toward them emitting an awful guttural rumbling which resonated throughout the space. He had closed the distance to about 10 feet when Nathan nudged past the line of men.

Seeing his brother's scarred face stopped Gavin dead in his tracks. He felt the change come over him immediately. His aggression melted. He wanted to protect his vulnerable friends but, seeing Nathan as he was, it shocked him and some small part of him broke inside. He crumbled to his knees and sobbed. Gavin found himself inundated, his head flooded with whispers and gasps. His proximity to his brother and Allura must have triggered something. He struggled to even breathe. Nathan was shocked as well; he hadn't even recognized his own brother at first glance. He moved to comfort Gavin but when he reached out to touch his shoulder it was smacked away. The attendants reached for their sidearms but Nathan waved them off.

Gavin got himself to his feet and composed himself as best as he could, wiping his face with a smear of his sleeve. That small act softened Nathan's heart; it was just like when they were kids. He was reminded of his little brother years ago, too upset to go on and too tough to accept consolation. Nathan smirked.

Gavin misread it as malicious. "So, now what?" The phrase

echoed in his own head. Repeated by phantom voices. Gavin's anger and desperation were evident in his tone.

Allura replied, "You are free to go."

Gavin was at a loss. He could not begin to fathom what this was all about. The guards began removing the restraints on Becker and Madson, then gently helped them up and two of them propped each man up between them. Gavin found it difficult to walk without wobbling.

"But then why all this?" Gavin was truly perplexed.

"We couldn't have you disrupting another meeting," Allura said, accentuating the word *another* for purposeful emphasis, then asked, "Now could we?"

Madson and Becker were hoisted up and out of the room.

"Where are you taking us?"

"Back to the van." She waved her hand in a shooing motion. "Consider it a gift."

She tossed a cell phone to Gavin. "We'll be in touch."

He clumsily caught it and put it in his pocket and stared at her in disbelief. Moments ago he was sure he would die here.

She sensed his confusion. "I cannot pretend to know or understand my master's motives. Yet for now, he deems it better that you live."

With that, Allura gently guided Gavin out the door. He followed his hobbled partners toward the van. Allura slowly closed the door, then, when the three men were out of sight, texted Xavier to alert him to their captives' departure. She then texted W to inform him as well.

LINKS

Oni had a boat waiting in The Battery to take him across the East River. He always found the water calming, and had anticipated the tenor of the Council meeting and planned accordingly in advance. His men were waiting on board a sleek speedboat. Oni boarded silently and stood at the bow. The engine purred to life and began to growl as it moved away from the dock and toward the Brooklyn Navy Yard.

As the boat skipped along, Oni grinned. The spray of water and the wind in his face, the sensation reminded him of simpler times long ago. As the boat slowed and eased into the dock, Oni sprang off the bow and briskly walked to a waiting Gator XTV. The driver pulled away before the boat had come to rest. Oni adored smooth efficiency and his men knew it.

He was delivered to a revamped shipyard where a myriad of vehicles and boats were housed. He had two dozen men on hand. Some walked the perimeter, blatantly armed while others were working on and around vehicles. At the rear of the immense space, crews of welders were busy cascading sparks from a massive two-story cage. Cell blocks that stretched the width of the space were nearly completed.

Oni strode up the industrial stairs to an office space that overlooked it all. He paused before entering and surveyed the activity with satisfaction, then clicked on the lights and removed his blazer to hang it on a coat rack by the door. A large conference table surrounded by chairs sat in the middle of the space. A small kitchenette to the right had a refrigerator and a small stove. Along the entire rear wall was a map of the Northeast. Seventy-six red push pins dotted the map. One for each Siphon he had sired and planned to collect.

COUNTER

Xavier had waited in his office while Nathan and Allura dealt with Gavin. He also did not think the time was right to reveal himself to the interlopers. Despite his fury toward them for their previous actions, Xavier couldn't help but think that if Oni wanted them, he had to keep them out of his hands.

He sat and waited in a melancholy slouch for them to join him. Nathan was the first to arrive. He said nothing as he entered and joined Xavier in the chair where they had first met and quietly sat beside him. Part of him wanted to share the experience of meeting his brother, but his gut and his ward urged stillness. The consequences of Xavier's wrath would be terrible. He witnessed it himself in Xavier's office.

As Nathan settled, Allura strode confidently into the room. She stopped directly in front of Nathan and Xavier and waited for some sign that it was permissible to speak.

"Yes?" Xavier asked with an annoyed inflection.

"The three men have been sent on their way in the exterminator van. I instructed them that we would be in touch and gave them a disposable cell phone so we may do so." Allura maintained a direct and matter-of-fact tone.

"The van can be tracked?"

"Yes, Sir."

"Very well. Inform me of their whereabouts once they stop."

"Of course, Sir."

Xavier sat cross-legged, his right hand covering his face. Without looking up, he patted the empty seat beside him in a gesture to have Allura sit. She promptly did so.

"Sit," he cooed, "we have much to discuss."

Nathan unconsciously wiggled in his seat and sat up straight, his hands on his knees. He had an unexplainable sensation that he was about to take a pop quiz that he had forgotten to study for. The room was silent for a moment and after an awkward and unbearable minute, Xavier sighed and sat up. He collected his thoughts and cleared his throat.

"Nathan, you no doubt had a surprising reunion with your brother. I would hazard a guess you both have changed considerably since last you met."

Oddly, Nathan had been dying to speak, but now found himself dumbfounded. His words would not come. He simply sighed and looked down at his own hands resting on his knees.

"And Allura," Xavier patted her folded hands atop her knees. "As always I appreciate your efficient and dutiful nature. Yet you must be wrestling with the possibility of very personal consequences if Oni is successful."

Now, it was Allura's turn to sit confounded. Xavier had stolen their words before they could utter them.

"I have been thinking about it. My estimation is that Oni will seek to displace me. It is obvious he is attempting to gain the favor of our Immortal brothers. His plans are both ambitious and blasphemous. I also believe he intends to claim The Source. It would be his right if he seized control. My fear is what he might do with it."

At that, Leto gasped and shuddered. Apparently only Xavier had thought that far ahead. One could only assume he was justified to worry about The Source. His lengthy lifespan had refined a cunning and tactical intuition.

"I must assure you both." He turned and faced Nathan. "Nothing will interfere with our goals." He then swiveled to look at Allura. "And daughter, anyone who so much as tries to lay a finger upon you," he looked directly into her eyes, "I will personally tear limb from limb."

Nathan gasped at the revelation and Allura simply nodded in affirmation. She knew in the very core of her being that her father always kept his word.

OPERATIVES

W hadn't had much luck in acquiring samples in the past. His efforts to collect any at Glen Spey were futile due to the fire destroying any evidence and the contamination from debris. Oddly enough, his collection was interrupted at the Cross home by Becker and Madson. He was certain that Becker hadn't recognized him. W had been wearing a ski mask and tried to hide his voice in a hoarse whisper of sorts. Eventually he would have to own up to Becker about that interchange and come clean about his involvement with the Gläm if he sought to work collaboratively with them moving forward. The notion of that conversation made him uncomfortable but it was inevitable.

He and Becker had met when they were just kids. Their respective IQs were the culprits. They both possessed stunning intellects tempered with a rational and unflappable demeanor. Even at an early age both men had quietly impressed their teachers and instructors. Their academic achievements and physical prowess landed them at one of New England's most prestigious and selective military schools. Becker was an uncannily phenomenal marksman. W was an elite fencer. Their admission was on full scholarship based on their test scores and athletic excellence. They did not become companions until after graduation. Both displayed an aptitude for technology and linguistics; computer use and languages came naturally to them.

As such, the Dean of Students paid them both individual visits midway through their Senior year. A recruitment specialist from the CIA offered them an opportunity to serve their country. They would get to "take out the bad guys" and make good money doing it. Most of all they would get to see the world while traveling in style. Becker and W agreed and, after some physical and psychological tests, they were immersed in six months of intense training. It was during this time they became friends; they knew each other back in school but were not close. The time spent together in training created a bond between them. They grew to trust and rely on one another.

Over the course of five gruesome years, they were inseparable and deadly efficient. Their covert and deft handling of volatile targets in the Middle East earned them a reputation as well as commendations. By the time they were in their mid-20s each had bankrolled enough to be comfortable and sought to begin a new life. W started his cleaning service wrapping up crime scenes legitimately for local law enforcement. It wasn't long until those committing the crimes noticed and appreciated his work and began hiring him to clean up. He quickly made enough to buy and remodel the funeral home. Becker was fast-tracked through the police academy and made detective in no time. Their meritorious service opened doors for them, yet they always remained humble. Humility helps to avoid undue scrutiny.

His recollection of the old days and the process of securing the Gläm tissue samples were interrupted when Allura called. W carefully slid the dead Gläm back into the cylinder that housed it, and answered call on speaker, while continuing to prepare a sliced section of soft tissue to examine on a slide.

"W, it's Allura."

"Yes, I know." W was fileting pieces of flesh from a scute of an armored shell. He deftly laid them on prepared slides as he spoke. Allura also had W on speaker so that Xavier and Nathan could listen in on the conversation.

She said, "As I indicated, our friends are most likely headed north."

"Yes, I took the liberty of piggybacking on the tracker signal from the van," W responded flatly.

"Very well, please keep us updated if you have contact."

W smirked, his gaze still focused intently on the operation at hand.

"Surely you could keep tabs on them yourself. Was there another reason for your call?"

Allura paused, silent for a moment. "The tenor here has become tense. It would be best if they remained uninvolved."

W's grin widened, "So, you'd like me to keep them away for a while?"

"Yes, until you hear otherwise from us."

"Us… Alright, understood."

Enthralled

The call was ended from the other side of the line. W chuckled to himself as he peered through a microscope at the samples he collected.

* * *

Xavier looked down his nose at Allura's phone to ensure she ended the call.

"That man is too clever for his own good."

Allura nodded in agreement.

LAMENT

As Nathan, Allura, and Xavier walked back to their respective offices it was quiet after the call with W. Each of them went to their office and unceremoniously closed the door and plopped down at their desks. The recent discovery of Oni's intentions weighed heavily on Allura and Xavier. Nathan understood what may come as a result but his melancholy was more so a result of his interaction with his brother.

Nathan sat intently tracing the burned insignia on his hand with his index finger. His gaze locked on the repetitive unconscious action.

"Can you feel them?" He whispered to Leto.

Who?

"My father and grandfather..."

Leto was still for a few seconds. *In a way, yes, yet I am them.*

"I know, it's hard to wrap my head around it."

At times it is for me as well.

"It's just..." Nathan exhaled, searching for the right words,

Enthralled

"so much has happened. They're all gone; first mom, now dad and Alice, seeing Gavin like that it felt like he was gone, too."

Gavin's appearance was dismaying to say the least. He most assuredly is still himself though.

"I get that, I mean in his eyes. He wanted to kill me." Nathan stifled a cough but couldn't suppress the sobbing that ensued. He couldn't hold it back any longer. Between heaves and sobs he managed to continue. "I think somehow I thought that none of this would get to him. That if I chose this it was on me. I mean we haven't been close since mom died but..." he struggled to go on wiping his now runny nose with his sleeve. "He's still my little brother." Nathan's sobs intensified.

He's still my son, grandson and brother as well. The emotional impact doesn't strike us like humans but we still feel the bonds our hosts have with others.

"I don't know, it just hurts."

It does.

Nathan's breathing calmed and he slowly started to regain his composure.

Can I tell you a secret?

Nathan chuckled at the suggestion. "What is it?"

Something no Gläm would ever admit.

"Go on…"

Every time we transition, every time we grow, we become more human.

DISPATCH

Oni was examining the map of the northeastern states which dominated the entire rear wall. Although the shipyard accommodations were not lavish they would more than suffice.

Someone knocked at the door and Oni commanded they enter without ever turning away from the map.

Daisuke, one of his trusted assistants, announced himself and quickly entered, closing the door behind him. He crossed the room and knelt down on one knee and waited to be addressed.

"Yes?" Oni asked.

Daisuke reported promptly, "The Suburbans have been prepared and customized as you have requested. They are fueled up and ready to disembark."

"What about the cages?"

"They will be complete by tomorrow morning. The first floor is finished and can be used. The upper floors are nearly complete. We've had welders working around the clock."

"Very good." Oni turned and motioned to Daisuke to stand.

Enthralled

"Call for the Suburban teams to meet here and we will discuss how to proceed."

Daisuke pulled his cell phone from his blazer breast pocket and texted the group. Oni went to a file cabinet and pulled the first three numbered folders out. Each of the 76 red push pins in the map were numbered as well. The numbers were an indication of the order in which the Siphons were to be taken. Oni sat at the conference table and Daisuke joined him. Within moments the three two-man teams were at the door. Oni motioned them to sit and slid the folders; one, two, and three across the table. Every team had a dossier on a Siphon that included a photo of them and a satellite map of their home address. Folder one was Gavin Cross. Folder Two was his daughter Clara. Folder three was Allura Thrallson.

"Each target must be acquired flawlessly. You mustn't be seen and any cell phones or computers must be discarded. These acquisitions are of the utmost importance to our plans."

At that, the three teams bowed and took their leave. Daisuke remained behind. Oni leaned over the table and spoke softly.

"I'm entrusting this to your supervision. Our plans must succeed; the consequences for failure will be severe."

ANTIQUUS LIBELLUS
SERVATOR JOHN THOMAS

Conjecture on Gläm Source

I'm trying to expand on what I've read from previous Servators and information that I've acquired in my research. It is my understanding that the Gläm are ancient. They are as old as the earliest forms of life on our planet. The research that I secretly paid cash to be conducted indicates that they were originally tube worms from the sea floor. These worms consumed material from vents on the seafloor. The theory is that they ate a form of Archaea that was sulfur-dependent but physiologically unstable. The archaea possessed an ability to survive by changing and adapting. An incomprehensible number of years of consuming this diet caused the tube worms to mutate or evolve into the earliest forms of the Gläm. The thought that most Servators have held is that from that point the Gläm continued consuming and growing while changing. The outcome being that eventually the Gläm found their way onto land and continued the pattern of eating and evolving.

These are the beliefs commonly held by Servators. Yet, my gut tells me that an integral piece has been disregarded. The research that I had done insinuated that these vermin reproduced asexually, budding off like a hydra. The sheer numbers of *pupae that circulate lend credence to the notion. There have been reports through the ages of fishing vessels hauling in Gläm to be dispersed. In my opinion, it would seem that a source of the Gläm must still exist. There are so many ancient tales of deep sea demons of an otherworldly nature. Beings like the Kraken, the Kilbit, or Cthulhu persist through lore. So perhaps instead of efforts to fight the Gläm on land, our time should be spent focusing on finding the trail of new Gläm from the sea. Although the extreme depths and pressure pose a major obstacle, if we could backtrack the supply chain we may then be able to find and destroy the source.*

REBOUND

Gavin was struggling to keep the van between the lines on the road. Whatever gas or spray Allura had used to knock them out was potent. That, combined with the shock of seeing his brother and all the voices he had heard in his head, made him loopy. Madson and Becker were stirring in the back but still couldn't seem to wake up. Gavin could only assume that his newfound abilities allowed him to wake before his groggy comrades. He was also reeling from seeing the scars he'd inflicted on his brother from their attack at Glen Spey. It would also seem that their efforts hadn't had an impact on the Gläm. It had only alerted them to a threat and angered them heartily. Gavin's head was swirling and he needed to focus. He really didn't know where to drive to. He instinctively felt the need to put distance between themselves and the Gläm. Despite the commotion that went down at the cabin it would have to suffice as a retreat. It was remote and the drive was a straight shot up northbound on Interstate-87.

Madson began to cough and stir. Gavin chuckled to himself

as he heard him grunt and fart whilst trying to sit up from the floor of the van. Apparently Becker was awake. He had been lying there, awake but still.

"Can you open a window?" Becker was not amused.

Gavin rolled the driver's side window down a couple of inches. He could sense that Becker must've been lying there trying to make sense of it all.

Becker's mood could easily be described as genuinely grumpy. Gavin was content to keep driving despite the tense mood brewing in the rear of the vehicle. Madson had tried to chuckle off his embarrassing return to consciousness but his partner was sullen beyond consolation. Becker continued to lay flat like a cliché Dracula and perseverate on the situation. Madson awkwardly budged his way through to the front passenger seat. He and Gavin resigned themselves to travel in silence until Becker chose to speak. They were almost to Albany when Becker finally sat up and spoke.

"Why did they let us go?" His tone relayed his honest bewilderment.

His question was heard but no answer was given. Madson was unconscious when they were released. Gavin was delirious and trying to control his rage. His reunion with his brother only further sent him reeling. Gavin tried to remember what was said.

"She said she would be in touch," Gavin intoned.

Puzzled, Madson asked what was on everyone's mind. "What does that mean?"

"She mentioned something about us not disrupting a meeting

and that they wanted us alive." Gavin was struggling to recall what Allura had said.

Becker was still lost in thought. Part of him was frustrated that they walked into a trap and didn't see it coming. Another part of him felt like it was his fault that they almost got wiped out due to an impulsive approach.

Mulling it over, it suddenly dawned on Becker, "We need to figure out what went down at that meeting."

"What will that tell us?" Madson asked, staring out the window.

"Think about it. They sent a team to kill us and bring our bodies to Forest Hills. By the time we got there, they wanted us alive."

Gavin was trying to stay focused on the road but he kept replaying the scene in his head.

"She said she didn't know her master's motives." Gavin paused, wondering if he remembered correctly. "I remember her saying that phrase or something like that."

Gavin's recollection didn't make the situation any clearer. The three men drove on quietly for another fifty miles, puzzled until they were near Lake George. It was at that point Gavin felt the phone Allura had given him buzzing in his coat pocket. He quickly grabbed it and tossed it back to Becker. It was a text message, presumably from Allura. Becker flipped open the phone and read the message aloud, *"Return to NYC unsafe, await further details."*

ASPIRATIONS

W had six slides prepared. Each slide had a sliver of Gläm tissue secured with paraffin. Normally one would want the tissue to be dehydrated, but in previous examinations no reaction had occurred using that process. His plan was to secure the larger scute sample in a Petri dish with agar and monitor any results. The slides were prepared in a somewhat unconventional fashion. After earlier failures to produce a reaction of any kind he decided to use what he knew of the Gläm to continue his experiments. Instead of formaldehyde, which he had in abundance at the funeral home, he opted for a saline solution as the Gläm were native to the ocean.

Next, he viewed the sample to observe cell structure under a controlled scenario. The cells behaved similarly to other animal and amphibian cells. W then took a T-pin, swabbed it in alcohol and jabbed an index finger, squeezed it until a drop of blood the size of a pea had formed and gathered it with a pipette. Then, carefully, introduced a minuscule amount of blood onto the sample. The cells instantly went into a frenzy, their membranes quivering and shaking excitedly, and abruptly opened and sucked the blood into themselves. The cells were still only momentarily and then began to writhe. Mitosis ensued and the replicated cells each developed and displayed a different structure. W viewed another slide that had not been introduced with blood and indeed the cells were fewer and smaller, then swapped slides and realized that not only had the cells multiplied but they also had larger mitochondria and longer endoplasmic reticulum. W compared the slides again to double check and they had absolutely changed. He surmised more advanced equipment would need to be procured to further study the Gläm cells. Yet he knew he was on to something. What that was, wasn't entirely sure. His hope was that if Gläm cells were able to synthesize and grow using human material that the reverse may also be true. Could human cells hybridized with Gläm cells regenerate?

SECRETS

Xavier was rarely rattled, but as of late it felt like everything was crumbling all around. It was difficult to establish a new territory and place a burgeoning Immortal in control of it. The last thing he expected was a power struggle from within the ranks of his Brothers. The timing of it all was less than ideal to say the least. There were the implications of Oni's desires to consider. His first concern was that his plans would jeopardize the clandestine way in which their kind has operated for so long. There was also the base nature of what he was suggesting; Machiavellian cannibalism, essentially. To add insult to literal injury, his own daughter and invaluable assistant would be threatened. Many Immortals had children but it was frowned upon. The reality of it was that the Immortals were Gläm but as they grew and changed they were not immune to human indulgences. The truth of it was that becoming more human was paramount to their survival but it came with a cost. Albeit taboo to father a child as an Immortal, most had a few. It was an overlooked transgression but nonetheless against the rules of the Gläm. In legend, Cronus ate his own children, except Zeus, in order to maintain power. Perhaps Oni was on a similar tactic, two birds with one stone, increasing his own power while eliminating a possible threat.

Whatever his motivations, Xavier would not allow him to succeed and would not stand by and allow his kind to be thrust into the public eye. Allura's safety was paramount and Xavier would not see harm befall her. There was also the audacity of Oni; it may be petty, but had he forgotten the order of things. He was challenging Xavier, after all. Losing was not his concern; while he didn't see that as a possibility, the ramifications of it all bothered him. He worried about how many of his Immortal brothers would be seduced by Oni's grandiose ambitions. His leeching of Siphons' powers was deplorable but did he also plan to blaspheme the Source. Xavier additionally never wanted to appear weak.

It was decided his next move would be best to visit the Baron. He would explain the scenario and then, with his blessing, deal with this usurper in such a way that it sent a message to the rest of his brethren.

ANTIQUUS LIBELLUS
SERVATOR JOHN THOMAS

The expanse of human history is a long and bloody saga. It was not uncommon for the Gläm to infiltrate the wars and feuds that erupted. The battles not only satiated their need to feed but also provided entertainment. Often, the Gläm operated as elite groups within campaigns or as mercenaries. The Persian elite guard were called Immortals by Herodotus after all. The most elite and elder Gläm, referred to as Barons, would broker arrangements for land, wealth and prisoners. Even at times lending their formidable size and strength in battle. Legends abound through the ages of giants demolishing mortal foes in battle. Goliath battled in the Old Testament. There were many Hibernian giants who terrorized mankind. Cenu were man-eating ice giants feared by Native Americans. Vikings were plagued by ice giants as well. Every continent has legends of giants. Many of those stories were the ancient Gläm.

The Gläm transitioned from battling amongst the ranks of soldiers as human technology and medicine advanced. They couldn't risk being detected. During the era of McCarthyism they saw an opportunity to move into politics. The accusatory tenor of the times provided a fitting diversion which allowed them entry as well as a means to eliminate anyone too close to discovering their secret. The primal attraction to violence that the Gläm feel so intensely is linked to their need to feed. The impulses work hand in hand. Although they were nearly uninvolved in actual combat they still maneuvered and manipulated to obtain the spoils of war. Within decades the Gläm had become completely interwoven in government and military leadership. Their rank and positions have allowed them to orchestrate situations and eliminate threats.

CORPUS

Xavier was torn and needed to walk a fine line between being cautious while simultaneously appearing to be undaunted. While also not allowing his Immortal brothers to see him as weak. Yet he couldn't allow Oni's plans to move forward. It was a game of perspective and appearance. Optics were essential to leadership. If he were to directly confront Oni it would send a message of strength but also of validation. If it appeared that he saw Oni as a threat in some regard it would legitimize him to their brotherhood. Amidst all of this he also needed to establish Nathan in a new territory. Not doing so would appear as furtive and worried. On the other hand Nathan would be vulnerable given the current climate of affairs which would thereby reflect poorly on Xavier if his protege failed or was taken out.

Xavier had navigated similar situations in the past but his gut told him that he needed to keep his people close until this played out.

Allura has been targeted, which would not be tolerated, and Nathan has undoubtedly been scrutinized similarly. Xavier sat at his desk, his mind swimming with myriad possibilities. He kept trying to imagine how the scenarios would manifest. It was akin to watching dominoes setup and toppled over in diverging paths. Only, the consequences were far more dire than he allowed himself to admit; he could lose everything and everyone he held dear. What he needed was an opening, an opportunity to act instead of reacting. His phone began to vibrate on his desk.

Oni.

Xavier smirked before answering and thought to himself that perhaps good fortune had smiled upon him today.

The phone rang three times before Xavier answered. Oni spoke first and oozed pleasantries with a hint of cajoling. "Xavier, I hope you are well," he cooed.

"Indeed," Xavier paused, he knew this gambit, and wouldn't fall prey to it. "What can I do for you, Brother?"

"It may be more so what I can do for you," Oni slyly replied.

"Really? Please enlighten me." Xavier couldn't help but seethe sarcasm.

"I'm under no misgivings about your objection to my plans. Given your connections, it is understandable but we must move forward. I've grown tired of hiding patiently." Oni paused for Xavier's response.

"You are correct. I don't agree with your endgame or tactics. No amount of discussion will change that." Xavier made an effort to remain cool and collected.

"Then we are at an impasse," Oni concluded.

"We are," Xavier firmly declared.

"Then I propose that you step down so that I may lead our Brothers."

Xavier couldn't help but chuckle, "That would be preposterous."

Oni was incensed, "Then I challenge."

Xavier had assumed it would come to this. "Very well, in two days time."

"The boatyard."

"Agreed." and with that Xavier ended the call. He calmly rose from his desk and he called for Allura down the hall. She came at once.

"Yes, sir?"

"Make arrangements for travel to New Hampshire, we're going to see the Baron."

"How would you prefer to travel?"

Xavier thought for a moment before answering Allura's question.

"By car. It will give us time to discuss and plan accordingly." Xavier turned and began packing a messenger bag on his desk. Allura stood motionless waiting quietly. He noticed she hadn't moved or called to arrange a driver.

"What's the matter?"

"Do you think it's wise for me to accompany you?" Allura paused, avoiding making eye contact with Xavier. "Given the circumstances as of late it may…"

"You will be joining me," Xavier interrupted. "I think you

may be surprised by Jēran and his entourage."

Allura nodded in agreement and moved in a daze. She had never met a Baron before and honestly wasn't sure what to expect. Now that she thought about it she rarely heard anyone other than Xavier even mention one before. The tenor of things had been tense lately, and not in the way she was used to. She had always taken for granted a sort of untouchable undertaking of her day-to-day routine. Her relationship to Xavier permitted her to move amongst their kind in a respected capacity which she complimented with her efficient and mannerly disposition.

"I'm not sure I understand," Allura responded, genuinely puzzled. "How so?"

Xavier turned to her with a smirk sprawled across his face. His countenance was fatherly and Cheshire Cat combined. She was texting their driver and moving down the corridor to the elevator.

"Jēran and his ilk are not unlike you and I."

Allura stared back at him, still lost. He sensed her confusion and continued. They stepped inside the waiting elevator.

"Jēran has children much like you and those children have children. You must imagine that his age is nearly unknowable, so as such he has had many families over the years."

"But I thought it was forbidden to have children."

Xavier laughed out loud at that.

"It's also illegal to jaywalk, yet it happens," Xavier made a gesture with his upturned hands, and shrugged his shoulders. "It is an indulgence that our kind has shown leniency for over time." Xavier smiled and patted Allura's shoulder with one enormous hand.

"Oni plans on consuming our progeny as a fast track to power." Xavier shook his head in disgust. "Not only is this an act of cannibalism which is most reprehensible but it also threatens eons of covert planning and patient strategizing." Xavier paused, his silence broken by an exhaled sigh. The elevator doors opened and a Suburban was waiting for them. "Either outcome is unacceptable," he added.

Allura climbed into the back seat. "I'm not sure I follow," She stated as Xavier settled himself before clarifying.

"If Oni succeeds I will lose my daughter and our kind will be exposed." He rubbed his hands against one another under his chin as the SUV smoothly slid into the street. "His impulsive gambit threatens all of us. I have no other course of action than to oppose him fiercely. Appearances also play a role; I cannot be perceived as threatened or weak in the eyes of the other Immortals."

A policeman on motorcycle glided in front of them turning on his lights and sirens and clearing their way to get on to Interstate 84.

Xavier continued, "It is also essential to get Jēran's blessing to demonstrate our allegiance and adherence to protocol."

ANTIQUUS LIBELLUS
SERVATOR SHERLOCK

Barons

The *imposing stature and appearance of a Baron necessitates their reclusiveness. In ages gone by there were stories of giant beings living a hermit's life in a cave. These were often Barons. Whether it be Nephilim, Cyclops or other iterations these Ancient Gläm have dotted myths and legends despite their efforts to remain hidden. No modern Servator has ever reported slaying one. More so none have survived any efforts to remove a Baron. The gruesome truth behind the tales of old is purportedly accurate as well, giants glut themselves on human flesh. Most accounts of giant beings from cultures across the globe hold this detail in common. This is yet another instance of the Gläm's base activity of consumption being relegated and diffused to cautionary folklore. All sugar coating aside, the Ancient Gläm or Barons have forgone the subtle form of ingestion of younger Gläm. They can quite literally rend someone limb from limb and gulp them down. As much as legend has dispersed the Barons' and the rest of the Gläms' true identity over time this theme of preying on humanity persists. Despite a tale's era or place of origin the common factor is mankind as a food source.*

DIRECTIVE

As the vehicle swiftly and smoothly moved through the traffic Allura was nervous with anticipation. Xavier could feel it emanating from her as she sat beside him. He had tried to ease her nerves through explaining Jēran and his family though his efforts were fruitless as she still hummed with anxiousness. Deep down he knew that she was internalizing the current situation and its perilous ramifications. Allura mistakenly believed she was responsible in some way despite having no control over her own origin or Oni's madness. Xavier wanted to calm her fears but knew she possessed his stubbornness and eventually she would need to resolve these issues in her own mind and in her own way. He thought that perhaps if she was tasked with something it would distract her a bit.

"Have you contacted Gavin Cross?"

His suggestion succeeded in snapping her out of the mental acrobatics she had slipped into.

"Not as of yet," she tersely replied.

"It may be prudent," Xavier paused to ensure she was engaged, "that he and his companions understand that their involvement at this juncture is ill advised."

"Yes, sir."

Allura called the cell phone she had given to Gavin. As it rang, Xavier motioned silently for her to put it on speaker phone. It rang three times before he hesitantly answered.

"Uh… hello?"

"Gavin, we wanted to make clear to you that you were to remain uninvolved with matters transpiring currently." Silence followed Allura's directive.

"Uh… okay."

Xavier began twirling his hand in the air in an agitated wrap it up fashion. Allura looked at him in bewilderment and ended the call.

Xavier looked at her in a scolding way while ensuring the call had ended by examining the phone screen.

"Allura, he was stalling. No doubt to track our location. That Becker is a crafty one according to W."

Xavier calmed himself and spoke in a comforting voice while patting her knee. "I know you are vexed as of late but you really must regain your focus."

* * *

Gavin continued to stare at the phone after the call ended. He too had put the call on speaker so everyone could hear.

Becker broke the silence. "They texted before, why call now?"

"That was the girl from the guard house at Forest Hills, I

remember her voice," Madson added.

"She was at the club too, with Nathan." Gavin spoke his gaze still on the phone, his voice distant.

They were nearly back to the cabin, the last thing they anticipated was returning to the city. Their efforts there were made useless quite quickly. Honestly, the men were lucky to even be alive. Yet each of them still wondered what transpired at the meeting. What events played out that would force the Gläm to spare their lives? Moreover, the circumstances seemed to have forced their enemies to keep the trio alive. There were matters at hand way beyond their comprehension. These kinds of scenarios drove Becker nuts. If he wasn't already agitated enough this kicked his mood into high gear.

"We've got to figure out what's going on," Becker fumed.

"They told us to stay out of it." Madson could tell his partner was wounded.

"But that's the thing," Becker paused for a moment, his eyes widened. "They needed us alive so somehow we're a part of it."

CAMPAIGN

Deep down, Xavier knew that going to see the Baron was the best way to achieve what he was after. It was also the best way to avoid squabbling with the other Immortals. If the Baron made a ruling, no one dared to question it. There were only four of them across the United States, and Jēran's reach extended into Canada as well. He was desperate to find a way to relieve some of Allura's fears but knew she would need to work it out on her own. She was just as headstrong as Xavier. For the time being, he was deliberating on whether or not to contact any of the other Immortals regarding his visit to Jēran. He thought that it may be wise to make them aware; in a subversive way it would head Oni off at the pass so to speak. His visit would indicate to his brothers that he was not taking the matter lightly but still following protocol.

His words about Allura's mental state had stung her. He hadn't intended to do so. She was watching the world outside the window go by as they cruised through traffic. Sometimes he was taken aback by her beauty. She was stunning and strong, stronger than she knew.

Enthralled

He wanted to tell her as much but he knew now wasn't the time. He wished he could express his concern for her well-being during these tumultuous times in a way that would resonate within her. Instead he had made matters worse.

At times like these, Xavier couldn't help but think of her mother. It was rare that an Immortal was impressed by a mortal person, but that was the case with Anastasia. They met when Xavier was procuring the property that housed his current headquarters. She was the agent handling the transaction. It was the 1980's and she was a driven woman in a field dominated by men. She was something to behold, stunning in an old-world way. Her dark black hair made her eyes look just as dark. He could recall the way she held her clipboard while touring the building and that, unknowingly, Allura did just the same thing. Funny that amidst all that has transpired he would think of that now. He resigned himself to texting his brethren to ensure his motives were transparent.

SUBVERT

Oni received the text from Xavier. He and the rest of the Immortals were all included in the message. The Gläm could communicate as a hive mind when in close proximity, but when removed from one another, distance creates problems with that ability. So, much like mortals, they resort to cell phones.

-Meeting with Baron

Xavier's text was succinct and to the point.

Oni was infuriated. He had hoped to avoid any involvement with Jēran. Yet he noted that perhaps this presented an opportunity for him. He contemplated for a moment how to respond. He wanted to ensure his response would elicit the response he was after.

-Social call?

Enthralled

He wanted Xavier to come out and admit he was worried, that he was threatened, intimidated. It would legitimize his endeavors to the rest of their Immortal brothers. Yet he would get no such satisfaction from Xavier.

-Protocol

was his response.

When Oni's strategy to make Xavier appear weak didn't work out, he began privately contacting each of the Immortals to sow seeds of dissension. His goal was self-serving in as much as he only sought to remove any obstacles from his path. Oni had become blind in his quest for power; it was "progress" as he had pitched it to his brothers. His machinations were more transparent to their eyes than he realized. Ultimately his efforts to garner support from them led to quite the opposite result he had hoped for. Each one of them came to the same conclusion, unspoken, but unanimously they wanted to stay away from Oni and his plans until word from Jēran came back. In the midst of all this Oni had forgotten that he was a whelp in comparison to Xavier. Xavier was far more ancient than he appeared and with his age came a multitude of experience and an abundance of raw power.

ANTIQUUS LIBELLUS
SERVATOR SEDLAK

Little is actually known about the physiological process that any Immortal goes through when they reach the rank of a Baron. It is believed that they are, and maddeningly, mimicking the appearance of humanity but far more adaptable and impervious. Hypothetically, as they advance in age, their physical form must also undergo changes. It is uncertain as to whether or not these changes are simply a natural part of their progression or if it is part of the adaptation process. One thing is for certain; when a Gläm moves to the stage of an Immortal after three gestation periods the physical change is drastic and alarming. One can only guess that, as an Immortal approaches the stage of development of a Baron, that the same sort of metamorphosis drastically occurs. From what is known of the Barons, they are giant, and immensely powerful. From piecing together various bits of folklore and legends, as well as more modern accounts, one thing is clear that their enormous size dictates that they remain elusive.

Speaking again, in conjecture mostly, we are aware that the Gläm all come from what they refer to as a singular source. But as time goes on, it would appear as though their kind may be growing in size and ability to be more so like the source that they speak of. The stories of their incredible size, speed and ferocity is only overshadowed by the intensity of their unimaginable strength. Perhaps it is much like the concept of megafauna during the Ice Age, where these creatures, in order to survive, must grow in size. It is commonly upheld that the origin of the Gläm is the furthest most depths of the sea and gigantism is also prevalent at those deaths. The crushing weight and pressure necessitated creatures to evolve as a means to survive. It may be that the long lived Gläm develops in such a way as a means of self-preservation.

SEANCE

Nathan had not been invited to the meeting with the Baron, nor did he want to join them. He remained in his office alone with Leto, and had been emotional after leaving the club. There were so many questions and few answers. His life as of late had been drastically changed and at a rapid pace. His presence was not necessary for the trip to see the Baron. He felt both relieved and left out. Honestly, he was glad to be left behind. He wondered what would come of the plans for him to branch out to Corpus Christi.

Best not to worry about all that now. Leto tried to calm his host.

"I'm sure you're right, I think it's just everything adding up."

May I help relax you? Leto offered Nathan politely.

"That would be great."

Leto began to gently secrete pheromones into his host. He felt Nathan's breathing regulating and his heart rate even out. In a matter of minutes he was in a deep sleep reclined in his desk chair. The connection shared by Leto and Nathan remained even in slumber.

Enthralled

Though Nathan was asleep and dreaming, Leto remained awake. Nathan's dreams played out like a frenetic picture show. Leto observed them with a distant fondness at moments where glimpses of childhood memories flashed. The meeting of Immortals replayed and was quickly followed by the incident with Gavin at the club. It was then that the dream began to unravel. His host's focus on Gavin's contorted face locked on and then began to swirl like a vortex. Leto was helpless, he found himself powerless to resist being drawn in. The scene became a fathomless deep. The Source loomed like an endless monolith above them. Its presence a crushing weight upon their joined psyche. Upon the midnight fabric of dream sea Nathan's charred hand clutched the Source after the explosion in the Berkshire's. It was replaced with the wry grinning face of Oni at Forest Hills. Then they were propelled upward at unimaginable speed. Immense volumes of water rushing past and around them. Nathan woke as he flung himself awake and sprawled across his desk. He and Leto both were gasping for air. Both knew they had been given a message, more so a mission.

It was clear they needed to protect the Source from Oni.

INTEL

Gavin noticed W's vehicle as he drove around to the back of the cabin. He alerted Madson and Becker with a sharp whistle and head nod. Both men became alert as he slowed the van to a stop. Madson slid the panel door open and approached the vehicle with his hand on his sidearm. He found the vehicle empty, W was not in the Suburban nor in the immediate vicinity. Madson looked to Becker who motioned to the cabin.

This all took place before Gavin had even exited the van.

As he emerged groaning and stretching from the drive, Madson and Becker both shot him a look of disdain. He remained clueless and shuffled his way to the back door. Shaking their heads Madson and Becker were hot on his heels.

"Hold up," Madson barked as he scurried to catch up. As Gavin opened the door Becker somehow slithered in ahead of him and was standing in the kitchen with his weapon drawn. W sat at the table alone sipping coffee, unruffled by the entrance, and catching Gavin off guard.

Becker spoke first. "Why are you here?" His gun still trained on W.

W sipped his coffee again. "Customer satisfaction follow up," he uttered before delicately sipping again.

"We're pleased, thanks," Becker retorted while holstering his weapon.

"Glad to hear it," W chuckled, "but you're not the customer I'm referring to."

With that W patted the chair next to him in a jovial fashion. Becker let out an exasperated sigh and hollered for Madson to come in. Gavin shook his head and moved to the sofa and plopped down. Becker and Madson sat at the table with W.

"Pray tell," Becker mused.

"As you may have suspected, my services have been utilized often by the Gläm."

Madson recoiled at the confession while Becker remained stoic.

"I assure you," W continued, "that I am not under their control, nor am I a host. Our arrangement has been, like ours, mutually beneficial."

"How so, may I ask?" Becker asked genuinely intrigued.

"It has been profitable in both finance and research. And, as well, the relationship keeps me abreast of the goings on of their kind."

This revelation noticeably perked Becker's interest and seemed to soothe Madson.

"As of late, there has been unrest amongst the Immortals. I

have been asked to ensure you remain uninvolved." W smiled and I tilted his head. "That doesn't mean you remain uninformed."

"Do tell," Becker chuckled while taking a sip of coffee.

RUNES

Xavier and Allura continued on in an awkward isolated silence as they made their way into New Hampshire. Both were absorbed in their phones, distant from one another despite sitting side-by-side. The driver no doubt sensed the tension. He did not speak to them; he weaved his way through traffic seamlessly and rapidly.

Soon they would pull off the highway, pass through Salem and head toward America's Stonehenge. A few miles beyond the enigmatic assemblage of stone, down a long gravel driveway, was Equinox Stoneworks. A group of contractors leaned against the sides of their trucks discussing business matters.

The vehicle rolled to a crunching halt in front of the gigantic structure of rough stone and wooden beams. Its appearance belied the homeland of its occupants. Fittingly, the massive structure would seem to be home to Thor himself. Perhaps Beowulf waited within sharing tales of his adventures. The sight of the place must have pleased Xavier immensely as an easy grin spread across his face as he exited and walked toward the front doors. The entrance was indeed impressive, double doors made of foot-thick wooden slabs and fortified with hammered iron stood fifteen feet tall beneath a solid granite threshold. Presently the doors were open, inviting customers to place orders.

Allura was slow to follow as the sheer size of the building undoubtedly had her in awe. Clutching her portfolio to her chest, she walked quickly to catch up to her liege.

Xavier strode forward with a jovial gate nodding and waving to the workers within. Allura was astonished, he actually seemed happy. Beyond happy, elated, his entire body language seemed different. His shoulders set squarely and he walked upright with a spring in his step. Normally he appeared hunched most likely due to his stature in comparison to the accommodations of city life. He was now nearly seven feet tall and elevators often vexed him. Also, most of his interactions with others necessitated he incline to hear and speak with people a whole foot or more smaller than him. Allura began to notice that the attendants at Equinox were all as tall and, even taller, than Xavier. Their expressions were just as joyous as they welcomed Xavier. It would appear as though this was a genuinely wholesome reunion of sorts. Allura was puzzled but pleasantly surprised to see Xavier in such high spirits.

The interior of the place was the size of an airplane hangar. There was a lane down the middle, and the sides were filled with neat rows of metal shelves which contained slabs of various kinds of stone. The massive slabs stood upright in six foot sections that rested in black metal frames bolted into the concrete floor. Allura and Xavier were the first customers of the day and undoubtedly surprised some of the men stocking the slabs in the rows. Allura gasped as she caught a glimpse of one of them handling one of the slabs as if they were made of cardboard. He swung it over his head in a nonchalant way and slid it into the rack. One of his coworkers tapped him to cease and desist but then they both realized exactly who had noticed them. Both of the workers laughed heartily and nodded to Xavier. Xavier laughed out loud.

Xavier laughed!

Allura was gobsmacked in disbelief. Her jaw nearly hit the floor and her feet locked in place. Xavier practically skipped over to them. He exuberantly shook both of their hands and pulled them in for a hug.

"Karl, Sven, so good to see you both!" He stood his hands on his hips as if he was surveying his homestead. In many ways he was. This was his home after all and it had been far too long since he had been for a visit. Of course, the dire circumstances in New York city necessitated that he come to call.

"Many times I was guilty of moving the stones the same way," Xavier chuckled. "'Can't have the customers seeing us swing the slabs around,' Jēran used to scold me."

Sven and Karl laughed huskily again at that as well as Xavier's imitation of the Baron's accent. Allura was still in shock, she was a ways away and both Sven and Karl peered around Xavier inquisitively. Xavier noticed their curiosity. He motioned Allura over to join them. It took a second for her to snap out of it and she moved sheepishly over for introductions.

"Gentlemen, this is Allura." Xavier extended his hand in a galant fashion. "Allura, these are my cousins, Sven and Karl."

"Pleasure to meet you both." Allura squeaked a response. She was diminutive in comparison to the three men gathered there.

Sven and Karl nodded to one another with a knowing look and a wry grin on their faces. Xavier picked up on their smirking faces, and nearly blushed.

"Well, I can't stand around all day like old times. Is the old man in?"

"In his workshop, like always," Sven half sighed.

"He doesn't get out much anymore," Karl added.

Karl and Sven suddenly had a melancholy air about them. They turned and led the way through the massive building. After what seemed like an endless number of rows of stone, they came to an office at the rear of the structure. The office appeared rather mundane, and most likely was where sales were finalized and contracts signed. At the rear of the space was a massive megalith-like stone with spiral ruins carved across it. In the center the symbol of the Glänt was carved. To the naked eye, the casters at the bottom of the immense stone could not be seen. Sven gently slid the stone aside to reveal carved stone slab steps, leading down into darkness.

WENDIGO

Gavin could see the steam rising from the deer below him in waves of pink and orange. The heavy smell of pine needles wet with a night's worth of rain hid his scent. There's an old stag amongst the group; he could hear the animal shuffling behind the rest of them. Its breath heavy, its shambling footsteps scraping through the underbrush. His enhanced senses were still sharp despite the morning mist. The angle from the limb he was perched on was perfect, directly above them. The deer would never expect something in the trees. The last mountain lion around these parts Gavin had dispatched personally. The majority of the herd was passing beneath him: one stag, some doe, and a few young bucks. The stag, the old one, its color not as rich and brown as the rest, in spots almost gray like an old man's beard. Its big eyes were tired and dull. At this stage in life he falls behind and lets another take his place. The fight has gone out of him.

The trees' leaves have turned red, brown, and golden and are falling off. Gavin pounced, the leaves beneath breaking the old deer's fall, as the momentum from dropping on it lands one square blow between its shoulders, buckling his legs. Below, the sound of its legs cracking followed by the stag's last deep bellows and then it falls silent as its neck snaps. The rest of the herd fled during the commotion. Gavin only wanted to let off some steam. He hadn't anticipated any of this. His primal transformation had taken over completely.

His exodus to the cabin had been confusing, exhausting,and abrupt. The Gläm had spared him for some reason and seeing his brother got to him. He was determined to try to push through all the questions in his head, lately he had far more questions than answers. He came to his senses in a small clearing between a group of pines. The dry needles crackled as he stirred. As far as he could tell he had passed out after taking out the deer and feeding. His face and hands crusted with blood. Deer hair intertwined in his stubble. Shortly after coming to the sound of mens' voices woke him.

He had wanted to experiment with his new found talents and it would seem his trial was not complete. It was dusk and he could hear footsteps and voices moving through the woods toward the cabin. They were unfamiliar, Madson and Becker were aware that he was out in the woods so they would not have ventured out this far without warning. He didn't recognize the voices he heard and he felt himself starting to change again, without even grasping the pendant. The transformation had just kicked in, the response was automatic, instinctual. The footsteps were getting closer, slowly he slinked upwards into a tree and was poised to strike. The last time someone had tried to assault him at the cabin they came in the cover of darkness and it was ultimately their undoing.

These men were moving in at sunset, three of them. The first one came into view, he was strolling casually down the trail, sunglasses, a leather jacket, cargo pants, and combat boots, but he was no soldier. From the look of it, he had an Uzi with some kind of suppressor. Gavin couldn't believe it, but it appeared that he was listening to music. The gunmen had headphones on, but not the kind one would use to communicate with other members of a group; these were simply headphones. He couldn't believe his carelessness, it had to be a ruse of some kind. Perhaps the other two sent this rookie forward as bait.

Although Gavin could feel the muscles across his shoulders rippling in anticipation he waited, and it proved to be prudent. Maybe thirty steps behind came two men who were obviously trained. They moved slowly and cautiously. Their gear was a mismatched combination of tactical and street wear but they moved with more precision and a calculated confidence. Gavin was pleased that he chose to wait if he had attacked he would have been torn to pieces. These other two men carried AK-47s and machetes on their hips.

In an instant, the tables turned on the man out in front. He was shot through the head before he could even get near the cabin. He simply dropped to his knees and fell forward in a heap; the other two gunmen immediately took cover. They hid behind trees on either side of the trail about 50 yards before the cabin and the shed. Both of the hired guns were focused on the cabin, trying to discern the source of the shot that had taken out their lackey.

Gavin was suspended above them in a tree on the right-hand side of the trail facing the cabin. He fought the urge to pounce, worried that there may be more of them coming. He listened patiently and intently, once he was certain there were no additional thugs on the way, he sprang from his perch. He drove both knees square into the back of the gunman. The force smashed his unprotected head into the tree immediately knocking him unconscious. In one swift slashing movement, he tore the throat of the man out with both clawed hands. The attack happened so suddenly that the other goon was turning toward his fallen partner only to look upon Gavin's gnarled and blood-soaked face. Then W appeared behind the last remaining combatant, the myrmidon was crouched, staring in horror at Gavin when W pushed a taser into the back of his neck. Sensing the threat was contained, Gavin began shifting back but struggled to speak, only hoarse whispers came out. W waved the taser side to side with a knowing look on his face. "Interrogation," was all he said, and began dragging the man by the back of his leather coat to the cabin.

MONKEY'S PAW

Nathan and Leto made an effort to control their breathing and compose themselves. Nathan was sweating and heaving, which only further accentuated the sensation of drowning he had just experienced. Leto had gone silent. He too was at a loss for words and struggling to process what had just occurred. Both of them were somehow immediately aware of the location of the Source. It was in Xavier's office and he was away visiting the Baron.

Nathan crept down the hallway toward the office. Thankfully the door was open. Most likely it was not operating correctly after Xavier's outburst. Nathan walked in cautiously; he couldn't help but feel like someone or something was watching him. Leto echoed the sentiment. Oddly, it wasn't as if anyone in the office was there watching them. It was more so as if they felt an incredible sense of anticipation. They couldn't describe it if they tried, it was as if the Source itself wanted to be discovered. The atmosphere of the office almost pulsed with an air of exhilaration. Nathan tiptoed around the front of Xavier's desk he mindlessly trailed his fingers across the length of it, the scrapes ran from one corner diagonally, a result of it being tossed across the room. Behind the desk was a bookshelf which spanned the width of the wall. Ancient tomes and artifacts were spaced in intervals along its shelves. A Viking axe on a display stand rested on the uppermost shelf in a place of prominence. Various objects of interest dotted the shelves: minerals, fossils and photographs in frames. In the middle of it all was the ornate box which housed the Source. Nathan could have sworn that waves of blue-green mist were emanating from it. Leto also noticed, and assured him it was a beacon of sorts. He had never experienced it either but something like instinct told him that that's what it was. Nathan carefully retrieved the box and gingerly placed it on the desk. He *creaked* open the lid and the visual miasma intensified. He paused regarding the scar on his palm and how identically it matched the insignia. He hesitantly pulled it from its resting place and the moment he touched it the entirety of his body went rigid. A voice like thunder boomed across his consciousness, Leto shuddered at the sound.

"You were right to seek me out."

The voice paused. It was like thousands of voices speaking at once it was deafening, almost crushing to experience.

"Oni means to consume us, the results would be catastrophic. We entrust you with our protection."

With that, the voice fell silent. The pulsing waves ceased.

Nathan stood alone, trembling. The Source, still in his hands.

"I'm not sure what to do…" Nathan felt overwhelmed and

lost.

     Leto replied, *Nathan, I don't think you understand.*

     "There's a lot I don't understand."

     Nathan, Leto paused, *the Source has not spoken directly to any of us in countless millennia.*

SOVEREIGN

W unceremoniously opened the door with his right hand and side-stepped inside while dragging the unconscious hitman. Madson and Becker were waiting on his return. Madson had a roll of duct tape and Becker was making an intricate knot in a lengthy piece of rope. Gavin was half-bounding, leaping and striding as he closed the distance to the cabin. His altered state diminished as he went, until he stood at the threshold of the kitchen door trying to get himself in order.

Madson slid a chair away from the table and set it in the middle of the floor. W dragged the unconscious adversary toward the chair. Madson helped prop him up in the chair and removed the thug's leather jacket. Becker tied his ankles together, and after a couple of loops, ran the rope up around his wrists. W tossed the leather jacket onto the floor and held the man upright while Madson began wrapping duct tape around his torso and the back of the chair. Once they felt certain he was secure, W began rummaging around in a small duffel bag. He produced a headlamp and a speculum. Madson was about to duct tape the man's mouth closed when W waved him off.

"Hold his head up and keep it still."

Madson moved into position behind the man and put both hands over the assassin's ears, tipping his head back. The goon groaned, beginning to wake from his stupor. Before he could regain his senses, W jammed the speculum into his mouth, prying it open.

The intrusion had him fully awake. His eyes darted around the room, blinded by W's light. He wriggled his head against Madson's grip.

W spread the speculum and the attacker's eyes and mouth went wide. He peered inside his mouth and down his throat, but saw no Gläm within. W abruptly closed and removed the device, then shook his head and indicated to his crew that the guy was "empty."

Gavin shambled in to join the men. The four of them stood in a semicircle around their captive. W knelt down to be at eye level with the intruder.

"Who sent you?"

The man blinked wildly. His eyes frantically scanned side to side in a desperate effort to assess the situation.

"*Eigo shabereru ka?*"

"Yes, I speak English." The goon acknowledged. Sweat beaded on his brow. The expression on his face betrayed his thoughts. He evidently did not expect any resistance on his mission. He also had not expected to tangle with men such as these.

"Then answer my question," W insisted.

The man remained silent.

W sighed and stood up. Looking down at the man, he crossed his arms with disappointment.

"You have seen me before. You know what I do for your employer. So there should be no doubt in your mind that I will dispose of you along with your associates if you don't answer me."

As if on cue Becker stepped forward.

"What is your name?"

"Taka."

Becker leaned in and rested his hand on his shoulder. "Taka, I understand that you do not want to share any information with us. But I assure you that you can tell us what we want to know and walk away from here. You can disappear and face no repercussions from your employer."

"Or we can just kill him," W interjected flatly. "From his appearance, he works for Oni and that is enough information for us to proceed. He is essentially unnecessary."

It was at that point that Taka shared Oni's plans for collecting Siphons throughout the Northeast. Taka also felt compelled to share the location of their shipyard headquarters. It was dark when they released him, scrambling down the driveway and down the road to the SUV he and his deceased friends arrived in.

Madson chuckled, then spoke, "That was textbook back there, you two." He pointed at Becker and W in a cowboy gunslinger motion.

Becker smiled. "Like riding a bike!"

Enthralled

"Are you worried about him running back to Oni?" Gavin's concern was evident.

"My services bestow a sovereign status," W grinned. "And I cut the brakes."

DECREE

Xavier led the way down the stairs with Allura close behind. His jovial gait remained. Taking two steps at a time, Allura struggled just to keep up. The staircase leading down began to bend around to the right; the walls were made of solid large fieldstones mortared in place and bathed in an eerie blue-green light. When they reached the bottom of the steps the floor was similarly constructed as the walls. Enormous slabs of stone had been set into the ground. Large pillars made of timbers interspersed the space at even intervals. The area was unexplainably dim and lit simultaneously by cast iron sconces mounted to the walls and pillars. There appeared to be some sort of smoldering stones within each that emanated the phosphorescence that illuminated the subterranean expanse. Xavier was undaunted by the scene and moved directly to the center where a gargantuan workbench dominated the area. Tools and bits of stone were littered across its edges. Crystals and what appeared to be obsidian glimmered in the gloom. There seated across from them was Jēran.

The Baron Jēran towered over Xavier even while seated. He was bent over a 10-foot rectangle of stone carefully etching a design. Xavier abruptly came to a stop and waited opposite of Jēran, politely waiting for him to finish the portion he was working on. Allura followed suit. They both waited, listening to Jēran humming a tune as he followed his intricate patterns. The base from his soothing song rumbled through them and reverberated along the stone floors and walls. He was immense.

Allura was astonished, as her eyes adjusted Jēran's magnitude became more evident. Seated and bent over his work he still was noticeably taller than Xavier. He was reposed on a throne of sorts made from solid limestone and it was as wide as a car was long. He filled the seat of the bench almost entirely. His hands were the size of basketballs around the carving tools he was using. When his carving was completed, he looked up to see his son beaming in anticipation of their reunion.

"It's so good to see you," his voice echoed through his chambers. "My only wish is that it wasn't under such dire circumstances."

Xavier sighed and bowed his head in contemplation, "Yes, my Baron, I'm concerned about what may come."

Allura cowered beside Xavier hoping to remain unnoticed.

In the same instant as the thought crossed her mind Jēran remarked on her beauty. "Allura, you have become such a striking young woman."

The comment seemed to fill the air and her mind simultaneously. She blushed, compliments were few and far between when you were Xavier's daughter. Again, as she had the thought, Jēran chuckled at the notion. Normally she knew all too well the thoughts and feelings of those around her but it would appear her Baron also knew. Oddly, she didn't feel as though the experience was an intrusion, more so she found solace in it.

Jēran cleared his throat as he straightened himself in his stone seat. He sat upright and became even more visibly immense than Xavier. "To get directly to the matter at hand." His voice took on an edge of severity. His very words felt crushing though he hadn't even raised his voice. "Oni cannot be allowed to proceed."

ANTIQUUS LIBELLUS
SERVATOR BECKER

On Pandora

In an effort to connect the dots, mind you, these notes are purely conjecture. In my reading of other servitors notes I came across an entry from a servitor who went by E.D. Sherlock, he was based out of Troy, New York, and I found an entry from the early 1900s that alludes to Pandora's box. It would seem that much of his work was analyzing myth and legends, folklore and fictional content that corroborated the existence of the Gläm. My particular interest was piqued by references to stories across the globe linked to aspects of humanity's curiosity unleashing terrors to our world. From what I have read, the Gläm historically played upon mankind's less favorable aspects. It would only seem fitting that curiosity would also be culprit in their machinations. In retrospect, so many tales allude to this concept; The garden of Eden, the fisherman's box, the raven and the pearl, the Hibernian cauldron. There are so many instances where the notion that fiction may be simply metaphor. It is hard to discern how far down

Enthralled

the rabbit hole is too far. Servitors are to transcribe the old book each time they take on the mantle; one can only assume that many eyes have looked upon the previous entries and thought similarly. My hope is that if there was a way to find the singular penultimate moment, whether that be infection, or in historical context, it would further allow Servitors to pinpoint the point of origin. I simply cannot shake the persistent idea that if there is a connection between all of them, and that if they share a common birthplace or birthing entity that if we were able to route it out, it would have devastating effects to their ranks.

FEAST

The first of Oni's crews came back to the shipyard. The poor girl looked like she had been homeless for some time. She might have been 16 or 17 years old. Two of his thugs dragged her from the back of an SUV. She had been blindfolded and her hands were zip tied behind her back. Oni had constructed a decontamination station of sorts directly below the platform that housed his office in the shipyard and had hired a nurse who had her own staff of two assistants. Their job was to inspect the Siphons brought in for drug use and any other illnesses or medical issues that would complicate their consumption.

This young girl, who went by the name Sadie, sobbed loudly as she was dragged into the area where the medical team began to process her. A large vinyl curtain had been hung in place but offered little chance for modesty. She was stripped down, her clothes cut away with scissors, and her hair shaved off. Sadie was shackled between two metal poles that supported the platform above and hosed off with as much dignity as cattle: then was toweled off and put through a delousing treatment, given medical scrubs and slippers, and was led to one of the cages that had been constructed across the back of the shipyard by two men who were armed with Uzis. Each of the cages were supplied with a cot, a blanket and a bucket for them to relieve themselves. Her tears quickly subsided to anger and she began to scream at her captors.

Oni and his team had not considered the possibility that their victims would turn volatile. Their concern with sedating them would mean that those effects would be passed on to Oni when he drained them. His patience grew thin after 15 minutes of the girls' unending protests. He had been trying to coordinate with his teams about other Siphons that had been pursued and, at the same time, had to deal with the issue of the team sent after Gavin being thwarted. His frustration was only embroiled by Sadie and her rather vocal commentary on her treatment and lodgings. Oni had had enough, the news of his team's failure combined with the incessant screams reached a breaking point and stormed from his office and strode to the girl's cell. He swung open the door and the terrified girl flung herself on the cot in the corner shielding her face with her arms. Oni seized both of her wrists in one hand and stretched her arms above her head. Sadie's eyes were wide with terror. His lower jaw unhinged and descended. The proboscis lashed out from his mouth and a mandible on either side of his tongue pierced and held each side of her throat still. The main stalk of the tongue bit into the center of her throat with the sucker ring teeth of a squid. Like a lamprey his tongue latched on and began to pump in an accordion like fashion. Sadie went limp, her eyes rolled back in her head and her life slipped away as her blood was drained. Oni slumped on the end of the cot beside her lifeless body. None of this had gone as smoothly as he desired. He hated inefficiency, and the first Siphon to be processed, had been a botched endeavor. He sat there lamenting how things had proceeded. Oni sighed and leaned back against the bars of the cell, he closed his eyes, in an effort to calm his racing thoughts. As he did so, he felt a wave course through him. It was as if a pebble had been tossed, casting ripples in his mind's eye. When the ripples subsided, he heard plainly his nurse cursing about *"the lack of sedation."*

"I told you fools! The sedative would then impair me as well!" Oni shouted from the cell.

The nurse came running to the cell door. "I know, sir. No sedatives were given."

"Yet you clearly said it was necessary."

"Sir, I never did," She wrung her hands, her head looking down at the floor. "I just thought it…"

Oni sprang up from the cot. He realized that her nervousness was because what he heard were her thoughts. She had never spoken aloud. He grinned and thought this wasn't all bad as far as things go.

"It would seem that despite our clumsy execution," he squeezed by the mortified nurse, "our first acquisition was a success." He left the cell and returned to his office.

BEACON

Instantaneously all of the blue phosphorescent lights in the Baron's workshop were snuffed out. Allura, Xavier, and Jēran felt a shuddering sensation as the rippling effect that Oni had experienced passed through all of their kind. It was utter darkness, all was pitch black and seeing anything beyond the tip of your nose was impossible. Jēran simply sighed in the darkness. He reached for two clear quartz crystals on his workbench. Hundreds and hundreds of years of routine allowed him to do so, without hesitation or anxiety. He took the two crystals into his giant hands and rubbed them together while breathing a word on them.

"Lumen."

The pale blue light in the sconces began to pulse at first, and then rose to a more constant brightness. As the darkness lifted, he could see the expression on Allura and Xavier's face.

"I felt it, too," Jēran groaned. "We all did."

Xavier's shock and awe quickly turned to rage. His face

contorted in an expression of sheer disgust which did not go unnoticed by his liege. Allura was bewildered; she had never experienced anything of this nature and magnitude. What Allura was not processing was that this event signaled to all Gläm that Oni had not only initiated his plan but that it had been successful. Xavier was teetering on explosion and was about to blow up. Jēran sensed his anger and decided he needed to take measures to ensure his protege could act in an effective and collected manner.

"Xavier," Jēran paused, waiting for his words to reach his enraged son. "I am sending Karl and Sven along with you to ensure our intentions are clear and our assets protected."

Xavier felt flush. His anger gave way to embarrassment as he realized his emotions had gotten the better of him.

Jēran reassured him with a smile. "By sending them it also sends a message."

"I understand," Xavier responded, bowing his head.

"Oni must not be allowed to continue consuming Siphons, and he must not take The Source."

DIVISION BELL

Allura and Xavier said their hasty goodbyes. Jēran wished them well. Karl and Sven were waiting at the top of the stairs. There was no need to explain the urgency. They made their way through the warehouse and out to the parking area. When the driver saw four of them, making their way toward the vehicle, he quickly jumped out and began flipping up the third row. From across the gravel parking lot, he could see the dire expression on Xavier's face and wanted no part of his scorn. Trying to comfortably seat three men who were around seven feet tall was nearly impossible. Karl opted for the front passenger seat, and Sven made his way to the third row, where he could sit in a diagonal fashion. Allura and Xavier took their normal seats, and in no time they were leaving the Stoneworks. Xavier began messaging his Immortal Brothers about the decree from Jēran. They too had experienced the effect of Oni consuming the young psionic girl. Xavier's message did not surprise them. Some of the Immortals had notions of allying themselves with Oni. Those notions were quickly swept aside after hearing that their Baron had forbidden such activities.

Allura opted to call Nathan; it seemed far easier to talk it out with him than trying to text. She explained that they were hurriedly on their way back to New York City and that the situation was grave. Little did she know that Nathan and Leto were all too aware of the perilous nature of current events. When she was finished speaking with Nathan, she texted W. She indicated that his services would most likely be needed in New York City and wondered how soon he could get there. Also unbeknownst to Allura was that W was at Uncle John's Cabin.

* * *

W could only chuckle when mere seconds later Gavin's burner phone buzzed on the kitchen table. Gavin read the text aloud.

"Be advised, hostiles inbound."

All of them laughed, the timing was perfectly serendipitous. They all needed a good laugh after the intensity of the interrogation. The phone buzzed again. Yet this time it was from Nathan.

-Warn family.

After Gavin read the message aloud the merriment abruptly ceased. All four men dispersed to call home in different corners of the cabin. Gavin texted Linda:

-Poconos

Enthralled

He hoped she would understand. After sending the text, Gavin went into the bathroom to wash up. Becker and Madson also contacted home to let them know they should probably check out the timeshare that Gavin had got for them. W had no family left at this point but he contacted his staff and made them aware. His funeral home was a fortress but forewarned is forearmed.

* * *

After Xavier and Allura had contacted the parties involved they sat quietly for a bit. Something was nagging at Allura. So much had transpired as of late, but she simply could not wrap her head around Oni's motives.

"What does he hope to achieve by doing all this?"

"Oni?" Xavier asked rhetorically. "Power most likely."

"But to what end?" The distress was evident in her voice. "Does he want to be a Baron?"

"He could never be a Baron," Sven added from the back seat.

"A fact that he seems to be in denial about," Xavier scoffed.

"He claims that he wants to move our entire race forward, but it seems more likely he is simply after his individual desires."

"So if he cannot become a Baron, why would he risk so much?"

"I personally believe he's gone mad and refuses to recall what transpired the last time Immortals battled like this."

"Atlantis!" Karl interjected from the front seat.

Allura gasped.

"Yes," Xavier's tone became fatherly and a touch didactic.

"Oni cannot become a Baron because he does not have Atlantean blood. More importantly, what he's doing shouldn't be done because of what happened in Atlantis."

"What happened in Atlantis?" Allura was curious.

Xavier paused contemplating whether or not he really wanted to get into recounting the tale.

"Long car ride," Sven added, "might as well."

"True," Xavier resigned himself.

"As it is commonly held, Atlantis was on the southern coast of Spain. It sat near the fabled Strait of Gibraltar. Where the statue of Hercules bridged the land and the sea. The Atlanteans were a race of people who were far ahead of their time. They had begun terraforming, and in the ancient days, their marvelous city was ringed with concentric canals of water. They were one of the few civilizations that actually seemed to welcome our kind.

"As we Gläm began to coexist with the Atlanteans, a discovery was made when our people began interbreeding. It's one of the reasons why it is frowned upon that a Gläm should have a child with a mortal. When we began to sire children that were half-Atlantean they were astoundingly beyond mere humans. They possessed strength and size that truly made them legendary. At that time the Immortals worked in a very close fashion and made rather calculated maneuvers. It was during this time that one of our ancient Immortal brothers discovered the same path that Oni is on now.

"Legend says that he allowed himself to succumb to extreme hunger and feasted upon one of these Atlantean crossbreeds and, in doing so, he gained great and terrible strength. He secretly began to coerce his own Immortal brothers into doing the same. Again, much like Oni is trying to do now. Oni clearly is forgetting the past, or even worse, choosing to deny that it ever happened. The bigger concern is that Oni himself is not Atlantean by blood. And once our ancient Immortal brothers were able to subdue and destroy those that were mad with power, unfortunately it came at the cost of the destruction of the Atlantean civilization.

"The resulting Immortals that were of Atlantean blood swore that they would not allow history to repeat itself. These ancient Immortals became the Barons that now govern over the Gläm around the globe. Every culture has myths and legends about Giants, Nephilim, Great Ones, Sasquatch or Yeti. More often than not, these are the ancient Immortals or Barons who have sequestered themselves around the world. They often lived in hiding due to their extreme size and outrageous powers. Part of the reason that they chose to live such solitary lives was the fear that if they were to ever band together, not only would it draw attention to them but also avoid the urge or temptation to try to rise up and dominate the planet.

"The goal of the Gläm has always been to be patient and to create a world more suitable for them and it takes time. Oni's ambitions will only draw attention and put our entire species at risk of being discovered and even being destroyed. So only Atlantean bloodlines can become Barons. For whatever reason our physiology allows us to exist far beyond the rest of our Immortal Brothers."

Allura couldn't help but ask, "So, is Jaren Atlantean?"

Xavier smiled and nodded, "Yes, Jaren is of the old ones and he runs the Northeast. Jaren is also my Liege."

Allura was deep in thought but managed to finally ask what was burning inside of her. "Are you saying that you are Atlantean as well?"

"Yes, as are you. My fear is that Oni's lust for power also comes from the knowledge that he never could become a Baron because of his lineage and that I was put in charge of the five boroughs of New York City because I could become a Baron. It isn't just a matter of lineage, it's a matter of physical ability, endurance and longevity. Oni simply does not have the makings of a Baron. I worry that he plans to try to make himself one by consuming those of the bloodline, or even worse, the Source itself."

CALL TO ARMS

"We'll have to take my Suburban. They are expecting me so they'll be looking for it anyways." W motioned toward his vehicle. "I'm pretty sure they're tracking the Exterminator van anyhow and you guys weren't technically invited."

"She did tell us to stay away from the city," Gavin added.

"What remains to be seen is whether or not it was to keep us away or keep us out of harm's way." Becker added, raising his eyebrows and looking at his partner. Madson was clueless, and scoffed, "I just got reamed out by my wife, so walking into danger sounds pretty good right now." Everyone burst out laughing at his honest appraisal of the situation. Amidst the laughter Gavin's phone went off. Still chuckling, he flipped it open. He fell silent.

"My daughter is missing." He spoke without looking up from the phone.

"That settles it." Becker sprinted into the cabin and began grabbing their gear. Madson moved to the van and began doing the same. W unlocked the Suburban and began to take inventory of what he had to work with. Gavin stood motionless. He stared down at the phone as if waiting for some kind of response from a message he never sent.

W hollered to him, "Go grab the guns from the other two in the woods. Cell phones, too!" Gavin snapped out of his frozen state and jogged to the woods. He grabbed everything quickly and moved hurriedly back to the trunk of W's vehicle.

Madson and Becker came bustling along, their arms heaped with supplies and weapons. W took the Uzi's from Gavin and ensured that the safeties were on. Gavin noticed that the leather jacket from the man they interrogated was tossed in the back. He decided to try it on to see if it would fit. As he did so he felt a buzzing in the inner pocket. It was a burner phone, much like the one Allura gave to him, he flipped it open.

-got kid, u get dad.

Gavin looked up at the rest of the crew, "They've got her. We gotta move."

INCOMING

Allura's phone went off.

-En Route

"W is on the way," she shared with Xavier.

"Good, good." Xavier nodded as he spoke. Xavier's phone now sounded as well as Allura's. Nathan had texted them both.

-They took Gavin's daughter

Allura and Xavier both were silent after reading the message.

"This complicates things," Xavier stated the obvious.

"It will be difficult to keep him away now." Allura was evidently concerned about Gavin becoming involved.

"Contact him," Xavier commanded.

"Gavin?" Allura asked, puzzled.

"Yes." Xavier cleared his throat, "This situation, though dire, creates an opportunity. By letting him know of his daughter's plight it makes it clear we were not involved. It also paints us as sympathetic supporters. Furthermore, it places additional adversaries in the way of Oni's ambitions. By coordinating with him we put ourselves in a win-win situation, he can help rid us of Oni and if he is killed in the process it removes a future obstacle from our path."

"Understood." Allura called Gavin on speaker phone.

Gavin's phone rang as the Suburban was already thundering down route I-87 South. When he recognized who was calling, he whistled to the car to get everyone's attention, and answered it on speakerphone. Allura spoke before he could offer a greeting.

"Gavin, this is Allura. We met earlier at the club in Manhattan."

"Yes, I remember. You were with my brother."

"Yes, Nathan. He is actually the one who alerted me that your daughter has been abducted."

As soon as he heard her say it, Gavin grit his teeth uncontrollably; just the sound of someone saying it out loud infuriated him. The thought of Clara getting harmed in any way, shape or form made something inside him boil over with rage. The last thing he ever wanted was for his wife and daughter to get mixed up in all this; he had hoped that getting them the timeshare would provide them a safe haven.

He responded, "Yes, my wife messaged me saying that she is missing."

"Gavin, we have not met. My name is Xavier and you could

say that I'm your brother's boss, to keep things simple. I assure you that my camp had nothing to do with this. We would never stoop so low as to involve children. I believe it may be in our mutual best interest to confront our common adversary together."

"I agree." Gavin confirmed what Xavier had been hoping

"Unfortunately, time is short. I think we should continue our coordination over the phone as we are moving toward the location as we speak."

W chimed in from the driver seat, "As are we!"

Allura and Xavier both were at a loss for a moment. They had not expected W to be directly involved in this way.

"Very well," Xavier replied, nonplussed.

"Intel is that he is at the shipyard," Allura pointed out.

"Can confirm, that is also what we have been told," W rapidly replied.

Again, Xavier and Allura exchanged glances as if to say, *how do they know?*

W continued, "I will text location, let's meet and discuss objectives, delegate who's running offense and who's running interference."

Gavin watched W motion in the rearview mirror to end the phone call with a gesture like he was slitting his own throat, then hung up the phone.

CALTROP

W arrived at the entrance of the shipyard before Xavier. The shipyard was a massive expanse dotted with shipping containers stacked high along the access roads, which led to loading and staging areas. Those areas ultimately moved toward the docks and the water. W texted Allura his location. Fortunately, he was familiar with the area and had an idea as to where Oni had been setting up. The bigger concern which immediately leapt into W's mind as he exited the vehicle was that every access point was a bottleneck.

W held his hand up to his brow, shielding his eyes, as he paced around the front of the vehicle. He surveyed the scene; three entrances fed into the lane they were stationed in. The narrow access roads, lined with containers piled two and three high, merged to a V. The three-laned portion, where they set up to stop incoming vehicles, was dotted down the middle with more containers. W assayed the situation and whistled to Becker while waving him over to join him.

"It's tight!" W motioned to the incoming paths.

Enthralled

Becker groaned an affirmation, and turned to look at the stacked shipping containers directly behind them. W turned following Becker's gaze and they both concluded the advantage would be gaining the high ground on top of the shipping containers.

Xavier and his crew came swooping in and parked diagonally across the intersection. W hurried over to the driver and pointed from the driver's side window to park beyond and behind the row of metal containers. He then moved to do the same with his own vehicle, parking it in a similar fashion on the opposite side of the access road. Xavier got out of the vehicle and was met by Becker, W followed suit after parking his vehicle.

W and Becker took initiative, years of work in the field, as well as the rapport they shared for as teammates, gave them an edge of efficiancy.

"We will take up position on top," Becker pointed to the containers, "to take out incoming."

Xavier was not used to being given directions but appreciated the direct and decisive manner in which Becker conducted himself. Given the circumstances he would let it slide.

"Gavin and Madson will position themselves on the ground." W added, pointing at either side of the row of containers behind them, "Here." Madson and Gavin joined the discussion but did not move in too closely.

"I and my brothers will move directly to confront Oni." Xavier said, indicating Karl and Sven with two outstretched fingers. He turned and took his leave.

"The plan is simple." Becker spoke to Gavin and Madson. "W and I will post on top the shipping containers at the entrance as snipers." He pointed as he directed, "Snipers up on top will incapacitate incoming vehicles and the ground crew can eliminate the drivers and extract the kidnapped Siphons."

Once everyone was in position the confrontation with Oni was the next step. Xavier was banking on Oni not expecting a direct encounter. The hope was that bringing the conflict directly to his doorstep would make escape impossible.

Allura was waiting for Nathan to arrive out in the open at the end of the road. For once he was punctual, the urgency of his niece being taken captive coupled with his revelation about the Source had him in a determined and frenzied pace. Allura jumped into the passenger seat and Xavier slid into the back seat with Nathan. Without saying a word, Sven and Karl stepped up on the running boards of the SUV and grabbed onto the roof racks to stabilize themselves. They simultaneously smacked the roof to indicate they were ready.

The vehicle slowly began to move forward down the access road toward Oni's improvised headquarters. In the rearview mirror Allura noted one of Oni's cars approached the narrow pass. They heard one of the front tires explode as it was shot out. Xavier encouraged their driver to accelerate in an effort to distance themselves from the ensuing altercation, he didn't even flinch at the sound, he was busy texting his brethren. Nathan was swiveling to look back at the source of the sound. Karl and Sven were undaunted and kept their gaze straight ahead.

"Tire-shot," Becker quipped. "Show off!"

W chuckled, "Still got it."

CHALLENGE

Oni was furious, he had planned on publicly challenging Xavier for his title and role as leader of the five boroughs. His timetable was to do so once he had been able to consume more Siphons and extract their powers and abilities. He was not expecting Xavier to arrive early and unannounced.

He watched, his mind frenzied, as Xavier rolled towards the hangar. The driver stopped just before the checkpoint and pulled the vehicle sideways so as to barricade any entrance or exit. Oni just stared at the scene in the distance.

Xavier texted his Immortal brothers from the vehicle.

-Baron's decree, Oni cease and desist.

Oni heard the notification, he slowly slid out his phone and read the message.

"It is now inevitable." Oni whispered to himself.

Meanwhile, the ground team was extracting a child from the

rear of the vehicle that had been disabled. The driver and passenger were escorted off to the side by Madson at gunpoint. Oni's thugs were being knelt down behind a shipping container, their hands zip-tied behind their backs. The disabled vehicle provided additional blockage of the access road. Gavin's adrenaline was pumping before he realized it, he was pulling a child from the back seat.

"It's okay," he reassured, gently guiding the child out the car door.

"Daddy?" The young girl asked. She had a bandana tied across her face and her hands were duct-taped together. Clutched in her hands was a teddy bear.

Gavin knew that bear.

"Clara?" Tears began to well in his eyes. He tried to speak, his words clutched in his throat. He pulled the bandana up so he could see her face.

It was Clara.

He could barely contain his joy. He hugged her close and assured her she was okay. She stiffened, still in shock from what had transpired. Gavin whisked her away and off to the side behind a shipping container. When he removed her blindfold she was wide-eyed in disbelief. He simply held her gaze til she realized just who her rescuer really was. Once she recognized him, she began to sob and wildly hugged him.

Madson took one of the goon's cell phones and tossed it up to W.

W texted Oni's group chat that had been ensuing.

-Return Captives.

* * *

Oni's cell phone chirped. He pulled out his phone to check the message. Much to his surprise he read the directive to return the captives. He heard the crunch of gravel beneath tires and looked up to see Xavier's SUV pull up with two large men hanging off the sides.

Oni was doubly shocked to see Xavier exit the vehicle. He was flanked by Karl and Sven and the three of them strode briskly into the hangar and past a throng of slack-jawed lackeys who just watched them approach.

Nathan brought up the rear and Allura quickly turned back toward the direction they had come, escorted by their driver. The plan was set, Allura was to distance herself from Oni just in case the situation did not end in their favor. Allura was furiously texting directives to their staff as she walked. Their driver had his sidearm drawn and ready in case of an altercation. She indicated that all available staff report to the shipyard to assist in freeing those who had been kidnapped as well as escorting Immortals to Oni's headquarters as they arrived at the scene. She strode purposefully towards Madson and Gavin.

Madson was standing watch over two of Oni's men who were seated with their backs against a shipping container. Gavin knelt next to a small child and Allura felt the girl's euphoric joy internally before she even got close. Allura immediately recognized that the girl possessed abilities like her own. She did not interfere with Gavin and the child, instead moving directly to the area below W and began relaying the situation to him.

As if on cue, two carloads of Xavier's men arrived, four men in each vehicle armed with shotguns and breach tools. Allura instructed them to refer to W and Becker for the time being and she moved back to Madson and Gavin to discuss how to proceed.

W and Becker directed the reinforcements to park their cars at a slant on each end of the disabled vehicle to further bolster the roadblock. Simultaneously the exterior of this end of the shipyard was teeming with black SUVs and sedans; the Immortals had all sent men to aid and assist. W passed a small set of binoculars to Becker as he pointed to the entrance.

"House of cards," W commented while Becker raised them up to his eyes. At the end of the road, Oni's crews of kidnappers were being overtaken and dismantled left and right as they returned with captives. Teams of men in black suits tore Oni's men from their vehicles and loaded them into waiting vans. The victims were ushered to waiting police officers. Local law enforcement had been engaged to comfort and return those who were abducted to their homes. Becker watched as the Gläm's media team was set in motion to control the narrative. Photographers and camera crews gobbled up photos and footage to supply the local news outlets.

"They've covered all the angles," Becker added while handing back the binoculars. "They've got their own spin doctors."

"I'm not surprised," W groaned, as he watched the entire end of the harbor become a chaotic buzz of cars and commotion. The racket was a perfect distraction for what was about to transpire between the Immortals.

Meanwhile, Oni found himself cornered in his own base. Xavier and his entourage were soon followed by an audience of Immortals and their attendants. Oni was now faced with no choice but to challenge Xavier in front of all his Immortal brothers.

Xavier had forced Oni's hand and they both knew it. Oni was trapped in his own makeshift prison. The irony wasn't lost on him or the other Immortals gathered there. If he raised so much as a finger against those assembled to thwart his plans, he and his men would be decimated. Yet the Immortals there were aiming to enforce the will of the Baron which meant he was to be stopped. He had no choice but to challenge Xavier, running was not an option.

The enormous hangar entrance was blockaded by a swarm of vehicles. Every exit from the shipyard was blocked. What few men Oni had left were trapped with him. Swallowing his hubris, he marched forward to the crowd of Immortals and their attendants. Xavier strode forward to meet him, flanked by Karl and Sven. Nathan followed behind, dwarfed by the height of the trio. Leto muttered intermittently about the prudence of bringing the Source along. Yet it was the custom that if a challenge was made, it was for leadership, and the Source was their symbol of authority. They met in the middle of the expanse of concrete, vehicles and building materials were staged along the side of the hanger. The stairs leading up to Oni's office were to the left of them. Oni's men followed behind him reluctantly and came to a stop, forming a semicircle. The two groups stood quietly and motionless for a moment.

Enthralled

Xavier smirked and nodded to Oni, the gesture garnered the desired response. Oni gritted his teeth and declared, "I challenge."

The two Immortals squared up to one another. Oni took a fighting stance while Xavier remained undaunted, cavalier with his hands at his side. Another calculated tactic to further infuriate his opponent.

Without hesitation, Oni surged forward in a flash, swinging a powerful kick to Xavier's side. The blow was executed so quickly it appeared as though Oni simply appeared at Xavier's side. The impact made a resounding hollow thud. Someone in attendance gasped. It had no effect, it was like kicking a tree trunk. Xavier nonchalantly seized the leg with his left hand pinning it against his own torso. For a moment he stood stock-still, he looked Oni dead in the eyes and in a lightning-fast response, he swung his right arm down in a chopping motion. The result was devastating. He struck Oni at the base of his neck, then drove his hand down and through him like an ax, splitting him from his shoulder down to the waist. The halves of Oni slowly tilted in either direction.

Xavier pulled his own hand from the torso while simultaneously shoving Oni off and onto to the concrete floor with his other hand. The resulting sound of the arm being withdrawn and torn flesh slapping the concrete floor made Nathan's stomach turn and his knees nearly buckle.

Most of those who saw it were aghast, holding their hands to their mouths. Whispers started to flutter amongst and between onlookers. While some just stood quietly in awe of how quickly and summarily Xavier had dispatched someone as powerful as Oni.

Xavier raised both of his arms in an outstretched beckoning gesture for his Immortal brothers to witness what had occurred. The circle around them silently grew tighter. Those gathered began to close in around Xavier and Oni. Karl and Sven, as they were the envoys of their Baron, both moved in to dispatch Oni. As they approached, they both drew seax knives from concealed sheathes on their calves. It was apparent they meant to finish off Oni by removing his head. They would bring their Baron proof that he had been finished.

The circle of Immortals and their entourages grew tighter still as they surmised what was about to occur. Nathan joined Xavier and stood by his side to witness how the Gläm dealt out discipline.

As Karl and Sven approached, a sudden burst of energy shot through Oni. His upper body had been nearly split in two. He scrambled across the concrete, like a scuttling crab, and in an instant had snatched the Source from Nathan's hands and was smashing it open on the ground. It all happened so quickly no one had time to move or react.

Oni smashed it open and slurped it down like an oyster. He began to cackle in a gurgling fashion. He pushed himself up onto his own two feet as Karl and Sven moved to finish what they had started. As they moved near to him, his torso could be seen knitting itself back together rapidly in grayish cords. Laughing maniacally, an odd guttural sound began to gurgle from his chest. He raised his arms to the sky, already almost completely healed. The crowd gasped and whispered amongst one another, a frenzied tension dominated the circle of

Immortals. Oni lowered his arms and leveled a steely gaze at Xavier, "You have not won." Oni raised an accusatory, pointing finger at Xavier and beckoned him back into battle. Xavier remained calm and cool as always. He simply cocked his head to one side, returning Oni's gaze and began to tap his watch in a scolding fashion. The gesture seemed to confuse and enrage Oni only further. He took a step to launch at Xavier, but as he did, the first bubble began to expand his throat. The left side of his chest and shoulder began to balloon out next, then his entire abdomen swelled to three times its normal size. Before he could take two steps, his body was riddled with swelling. Within seconds his face became featureless, his hands so swollen his fingers were not distinguishable. He began to writhe and shake, his body trembled. As he tried to close the distance between them his body had become a quivering mass of bloated, twisted tissue. His skin stretched to the breaking point, began to rupture and ooze its contents out onto the floor. In a matter of mere moments, he had become a revolting mound of flesh.

"*Yokai!*" one of Oni's men shouted. "*Nuppeppo!*" another cried as they backed away.

As if possessed by a never before seen courage Nathan stepped forward and without hesitation drove his arm into the quivering mass of what had been Oni. He twisted his arm within and wrenched out the piece of the Source and gingerly tried to place it back within the reliquary. His actions did not go unnoticed and those gathered nodded and whispered their approval. Even Xavier was impressed with his resolve.

Karl and Sven gently took the talisman from Nathan.

"Our Baron will repair it," Sven said bowing.

"What of his remains?" Karl asked Xavier.

"Burn it!" Xavier exclaimed. "I will deliver the ashes to our Baron personally."

OPENING

Xavier had spoken and the remaining Immortals dared not question his orders. Even his closest allies were shocked at how formidable he was. Everyone knew he wasn't to be trifled with, but the events of the day absolutely confirmed the notion.

Karl and Sven left the gathering to search for a gas can to incinerate Oni's corpse. Xavier called the Immortals to him to discuss. As they gathered not 20 feet away from the scene of the fight, their attendants began dispatching staff so they could clean and clear the area before reporting home for further debriefing. A blaze rose up in a woosh of air behind them.

The leaders of the burroughs waited for Xavier to speak.

"The only conclusion we can all agree on is that this matter is resolved," Xavier said to the Immortals, who all nodded in agreement. "And the path Oni sought is never to be pursued again." Again, all gathered agreed, even those that seemed tempted by Oni's diatribe at the meeting. "The next matter to discuss is the vacancy created with

Oni gone." Xavier's gaze moved to Nathan who stood watch over the blaze. "I have a recommendation for a successor." His Immortal brothers deduced what he was insinuating. Although the role was usually reserved for Immortals, Nathan had been groomed to take over an expanded territory down South. It would take little convincing given all that had occurred. Xavier's handling of the situation had sent a very clear message.

Moments later Allura joined them accompanied by Becker, W, and Madson. Gavin and Clara strolled behind, lost in each other's company. Gavin had Linda on speaker phone and was arranging to drop off his daughter after a well-deserved Happy Meal at McDonald's on the way home. The team's spirits were high and, upon their arrival, Xavier excused himself from his brothers and beckoned everyone to join him in what had been Oni's office.

Everyone settled around the table. Xavier stood looking at the map that covered the rear wall of the office. He had his back to the group gathered there. His hands clasped behind him, he leaned forward examining the photos of Siphons pinned there, then turned to address the Immortals.

"Nathan, welcome to your new base of operations. Although it is not luxurious it will work as you transition into leadership."

Nathan was puzzled, "What about Texas?"

"I've made arrangements to cover the expansion." Xavier turned his attention to Allura. "We will need to ensure the media portrays today's events as the dismantling of a human trafficking operation. Paint local law enforcement as heroes, of course, to prevent further curiosity." Allura nodded and began texting her contacts.

The notion ruffled Becker, who asked, "Why are we here, Sir?"

"Two reasons," Xavier wasted no time responding, "First, my thanks for your assistance. Your services will be required in wrapping all this up." Xavier swirled his hand in a circular motion. "We will need to reconcile with each abductee and offer monetary compensation to each of them. Also, all of this information," he waved an arm at the map, "should be collected and processed accordingly. Allura, I'll leave the matter to you and Nathan with the assistance of W." Xavier walked slowly away from the head of the conference table and to the door. He grasped the handle and spoke, "Lastly, our alliance has come to a close. Any interference in our operations will not be tolerated." He sighed, opening the door. "I am in need of rest and must retire."

With that, Xavier exited and made his way through the hangar, into a waiting vehicle. Becker, Madson, and Gavin, along with Clara, excused themselves. Allura had arranged a driver for them.

W took Allura by the arm and pulled her out of earshot from the others. He said to her, just above a whisper, "We need to talk. Oni's office in five minutes."

Nathan ambled over to Gavin as he left, the two stared at each other in an awkward moment of sentiment and simply shook hands before parting ways. As they walked down the stairs, Allura's office staff trudged past them going back up, carrying file boxes to collect all of Oni's things.

A celebratory McDonald's stop on the interstate found the

foursome surprised as the driver, who spoke very little to them as they exited the city, covered the cost at the drive-through. As Clara nibbled nuggets, Gavin texted Linda their estimated time of arrival. He waited for a response, staring at the phone while mindlessly chomping down a cheeseburger in four bites. They were all famished and spoke little as they wolfed down their food. Gavin shoved a handful of fries in his mouth; his eyes still transfixed on the phone screen. Still no response, he checked if it had truly been sent, it had been delivered, no reply.

His mind swirled with possibilities. Was she okay? Maybe she was busy getting things together for a celebration? This could be it. This could be the moment that reunites them. Gavin imagined her tidying the house, decorating the front door, and pacing the living room giddy with joy. He pictured Linda rushing to the vehicle and hugging him and Clara, begging him to stay the night. Things would be better now, Linda would see that these things were beyond his control, but that they could be a family again. If they stayed strong and vigilant maybe it could work. If only he could make Linda see that it wasn't his fault.

He shoveled in the last of the fries and slurped his Dr. Pepper. The phone was silent, it would remain that way.

Clara leaned against him and nodded off. He quietly sighed and pocketed the phone. He knew he was deluding himself, deep down he knew. This would have to be enough, this moment, his daughter with him dozing against his arm, she was safe. This brief snippet of a life. A life he would have to let go of. It was too much to bear. He wanted it so badly but it was evident from what happened to Clara that

227

he posed a threat to those he loved most. He needed them to be part of his life, more than anything, but ultimately he couldn't ensure their safety. He could only hope Linda might take a chance on him, again.

Gavin had hoped for a hero's welcome when he reunited his daughter and her mother. Linda ran to the car before it had even stopped in the driveway. She tore open the door, her face reddened as she had obviously been sobbing. Linda scanned the interior frantically, reached in, and scooped Clara up in her arms.

"Linda," Gavin began to speak. Linda glared fiercely at her estranged husband. She had no tears now. Her face was full of rage as she snatched Clara up in her arms and walked to the house. She had no words for Gavin. Her expression told Gavin that "this was his fault." He made no effort to chase her down and explain. The car was silent as they continued their journey north. What could anyone really say to comfort him? A mother's reaction to such a scenario could have gone much worse. As they got closer to North Creek, W texted.

-Call after drop off

Once they bid the driver adieu at the cabin Becker called W on speaker phone.

"No time. Listen." The three men craned their necks to listen intently. "Sending photos of map, propose creating a network."

And with that, W hung up.

"What does he mean by 'network?'" Madson asked.

"The Siphons," Becker responded.

"They're going to need our help," Gavin added, "especially now that the Gläm know about them."

"What about Xavier's warning?" Madson suggested cautiously

"We all heard what he said," Becker quipped and proceeded to open his laptop to examine the images.

RESOURCES AND RESPONSIBILITY

Allura glanced around furtively as she entered Oni's office, sensing W's apprehension before even opening the door. He had obviously been caught with his hand in the proverbial cookie jar. She had a sense that he was hiding something but wasn't clear on what his intentions were. His duplicity as of late had her seriously questioning his effectiveness under their employment. Yet his track record was sterling and his results were top-notch. She couldn't understand it, but deep down she liked him. The rationale was unknown; just that in her gut she trusted him despite her recent misgivings.

"What are you up to?" She was surprised at how direct she just was.

W knew he was caught and given everything that had transpired in the past day or so he decided to play it coy. He slid his cell phone into his breast pocket.

"Whatever do you mean?" He smiled wryly.

"Let's cut to the chase." Allura put her hands on her hips blocking the door. She posed no threat and would not serve as much of a blockade. Yet she had little patience after the day's events and was mentally exhausted.

W could tell by the expression on her face that perhaps it was time to come clean. He had been tap dancing on both sides of things for a while now and, in this moment, he saw an opportunity. An opportunity not only to divulge his true intentions, but also perhaps to solidify an ally. He nodded an acquiescence to all and walked over to the bistro-style kitchen area and began to make two K-cups of coffee. Without saying a word, he pulled out a chair at the conference table and, with a pleading look in his eyes, motioned for her to join him.

Allura let out an exasperated sigh and shuffled to the seat he had pulled out for her. W retrieved the coffees and rejoined her. He sat himself down and begged the question, "Do you want to know why?"

"Why what?" Allura was genuinely puzzled.

"Why all this?" W waved his hands around in a circular fashion. "Why get involved? Why stick my neck out? Why work both sides of the situation?" W was a little bit in disbelief with his own willingness to share. He was only apprehensive for an instant. Unbeknownst to him, Allura was exuding her charm on him. Oddly, she never really had to think about using it, in instances like this it just manifested.

"I lost someone very dear to me." He paused for a moment collecting himself. "I did my tours in the Middle East and came back home. When I got back my folks shared the news that my little sister was dying. She was fighting muscular dystrophy and losing the battle. I was beside myself and couldn't understand why they hadn't told me. When she passed it sent me into a dark place and I fell into some bad habits and some nasty clandestine work. The money came easy, but sleep, peace, and hope had vanished. I resigned myself to the abyss. This continued until I first encountered the Gläm. While initially it was just a hunch, I had a strong belief that something was different. as I learned more I grew hopeful."

"What were you hoping for?" Allura interjected then sipped her coffee.

"A solution…"

"For what?"

"For dying, disease, pain, and suffering. I don't suspect your kind would process the potential for good your amazing physiology contains. I'm not foolish enough to delude myself that there is an ounce of altruism in your motivations. Yet, the capabilities for healing and saving people from the withering fate my sister Hannah endured are staggering. I've been researching, gathering, and using samples from the scenes I've cleaned. The results are insufficient and in need of further findings. The implications," W exhaled for emphasis, "they're boundless."

"Are you suggesting experimenting on Gläm?" Allura asked, clearly vexed.

"Heaven's no!" W raised his hands in a halting gesture. "Of course, samples of blood and tissue will be needed for study. I would propose that our current predicament provides an opportunity that I would like to discuss further with you."

"I'm intrigued, go on." She was curious yet uncertain.

"I worry what will be done with the information that Oni gathered. Do you have any inclinations?"

"My assumption is that it will be gathered and destroyed. Siphons have always been considered a *dirty little secret.*"

"So, what if instead of your staff lugging it back to be shredded, they simply put it in the back of my car and I deal with it?"

"They haven't left the premises. What are you planning to do with it?" She took out her phone and was poised to message her staff.

"My plan isn't fully realized. Suffice it to say, I plan on attempting to create a support system for them and provide a safe haven."

* * *

Nathan walked the interior of the hangar with Daisuke, Oni's former assistant. Clipboard in hand, he was attempting to take notes on the assets that were present. He was a "numbers guy" and often he found himself wishing that everything else was as orderly. Yet, here he was taking inventory of vehicles and vessels, construction equipment, and property. He was grateful for Daisuke's willingness to assist him given the circumstances. After they had made a preliminary circuit of the interior, Nathan handed off the clipboard to Daisuke to continue a sweep of the grounds. Nathan headed up to the office in hopes of accessing any physical or electronic files that might help him garner some sense of Oni's holdings.

As he entered, the tension in the room was obvious. W and

Enthralled

Allura were seated across from one another and it was evident that they were engaged in a discourse of some sort.

"May I come in?" He stood awkwardly with the door half open.

"Of course," Allura replied. "Your timing is impeccable."

"Really? How so?" Nathan made his way to the kitchenette for a bottle of water. Leto was not fond of hot beverages. He cracked open the bottle and seated himself.

"W has a proposal." Allura gestured to W with an upturned hand.

"I'm all ears." Nathan reclined and crossed his legs.

"I'm suggesting you release the documents pertaining to Oni's Siphon progeny to my charge."

"To what end? What do you gain from doing so?" Nathan's interest was roused.

"Only to offer them sanctuary and a place in this world." W offered as clarification.

"Are you certain it isn't primarily to experiment on them?" Allura interrupted sharply.

"Again, I could discover a great deal that would aid in my research but would only proceed with those who voluntarily offered assistance." W's ire was rising. Allura's implications were less than flattering.

"So, from a business standpoint, all you want are the documents, you are not asking for any financial or personnel support?" Nathan resorted to brass tacks.

"No, for a few reasons. First, no connections to your organization. The lack of a paper trail will allow for your camp's plausible deniability. Second, I do not wish to be beholden to you or yours in this endeavor. My thought is that as the victims are approached for restitution my services could be offered as a resource for those interested." W waited for their response.

"Essentially, we were tasked," Nathan motioned to Allura, "with the removal of these documents as a means to make way for me moving in and they were to be disposed of. So, I see no problem with you, as our cleaner, taking them. Plausible deniability as you mentioned. I trust that Allura would concur."

Allura nodded and added, "I will require a modicum of contact to ensure their proper care. I am, after all, amongst their ranks." Allura hit send on her text message to her staff.

W stood up from his seat, "Thank you for your help." He turned to leave, but then stopped short. "Oh, and I want the map as well."

W waited patiently as the materials were loaded in before jumping in and heading out of the city. Once he was on the Taconic, he called Becker. The phone rang and he picked up after two rings.

"Got a minute?" He asked tentatively.

"What's up?" Becker was apparently back at the cabin; he could hear Madson in the background consoling Gavin.

"Can you put me on speaker?" Becker moved to the kitchen table and plopped the phone in the center.

"Ok, so I have all the records and the map from Oni's office.

Enthralled

I negotiated with Allura and Nathan to allow me to take them. The plan was that they were going to allegedly destroy the documents. Even if that were true, I didn't want to risk all of that information being in their hands. Especially after seeing what they did. They came after Gavin and even kidnapped his daughter, so I proposed that I would take the documents and try to reach out to other Siphons that may be in need of assistance or a safe place to live. What I'm proposing is this; we create a homestead of sorts so that these folks can try to figure out not only a way to live but also a safe place to try to figure out what they're capable of. My property is already secure. I have surveillance as well as the funds and the staff to assist in establishing it. The big question is whether or not you guys want in?"

* * *

The cabin was quiet. The men gathered around the table, were at a loss for words. Even Becker, who knew W better than the rest, was beyond surprised at his humanitarian suggestion.

"I'm in," Gavin was the first to break the silence, "I don't want what happened to Clara to happen to anyone else ever again, and my father left me a very large amount of money when he passed, money that I've barely even scratched the surface of."

Madson chimed in next. "I'm really close to retirement. What are we talking about here?"

Becker added, "Technically I can retire anytime I want."

They couldn't see it, but W was smiling. "It sounds like if we're all in agreement. Now it's just a matter of logistics. I asked Nathan and Allura if they could offer my contact information to families who were interested when they made their rounds offering restitution to those who were abducted. I'm on my way to you so that we can try to sort this out."

W hung up the call, and Gavin started to get a pot of coffee brewing. Becker went to retrieve his laptop and get it set up at the table. The four of them would work to the wee hours of the morning, the foundations of what was to become known as the Cross Haven had been set into motion.

REALIZATION

A few days after the dust settled, things felt a little more normal. Nathan had begun to establish himself as the new sovereign of Oni's territory. It would take time, change is inevitable and always uncomfortable. Xavier was back at the office with Allura and was ensuring everything was in order as he prepared for a trip to see his Baron.

"Where is the case I requested?" Xavier asked with his back turned to her as he was scrolling through his schedule.

"I have it here." Allura was standing not six feet behind him. She held a wooden crate with handles on the sides. It looked larger and heavier than reality said it should in her small hands.

Xavier turned and took the crate abruptly. He set it on his desk and lifted the hinged lid. After pushing aside a section of raffia ribbon he revealed the lid of an urn, then withdrew it from the packing material and held it aloft. The black lacquered urn had a brass plate set into it inscribed with *Oni* on it. Satisfied, he gently placed it back into the crate and closed the lid.

"Have you arranged a driver?"

"Yes, they are waiting in the parking garage." Allura couldn't discern what had Xavier so vexed.

"Very good." He snatched up the crate and moved quickly down the hall with Allura trying desperately to keep up. He stopped at the entrance to the elevator waiting for it to arrive. Allura moved to stand beside him. He sighed at her arrival.

"You cannot accompany me," Xavier grumbled. "I'm sorry."

Allura was thunderstruck. She was always at Xavier's side. What was different about this trip? She offered no protest or inquiry. She simply and solemnly turned and walked back to her office. She heard the elevator chime as it arrived. Xavier left with no further comment or explanation.

The ride to the Baron was quiet. Xavier was lost in thought, his head was swimming with doubt and regret. He had initially felt proud after dispatching Oni. Now he wondered if it could have been avoided, if it was necessary that things went so far. He questioned his leadership and personal involvement due to Allura. He was piling the onus of everything that had transpired onto himself.

Karl and Sven greeted him as he entered Equinox. The place was busy with customers. The three men glided past them and into the back office. Karl closed the door behind them as Sven slid the stone aside. Xavier descended the staircase and approached Jēran at his workstation. He held the box containing the urn until his liege finished the portion of the design he was carving. When Jēran looked up, he motioned for Xavier to put it down. Jēran gingerly opened the crate and removed the urn. It looked tiny in his hands, he held it up closely to his face to read the inscription.

"You've done well," Jēran replaced the urn and leveled his gaze at Xavier. "So why are you so distraught?"

"I keep questioning if I had done something differently, perhaps Oni could have been spared."

"Did you give him the idea? Did you not warn him?" Jēran asked rhetorically.

"No, in retrospect I see it as a loss of one of our Brothers. In the moment I simply wished him gone. Yet now I worry that…"

"Worry is a mortal vice." Jēran cleared his throat and began again, "I am actually rather pleased. After so many, many years I am excited for change. I haven't been surprised in such a long time."

"Surprised?" Xavier asked, "By what?"

"Your protege," Jēran replied.

"How so?"

"No one has interacted directly with Source since the battle of Atlantis. It would seem that the explosion at Glen Spey somehow linked them together." With that Jēran reached into a drawer and withdrew the talisman that housed the Source. He handed it to Xavier, who bowed while taking it from him.

"Don't trouble yourself with things outside of your control. The blast at the ceremony connected Nathan to our Source and Oni's transgression led to Nathan taking his place." Jēran paused for a moment for emphasis. "We may be ancient but we are not omnipotent."

Acknowledgements

First, let me express my sincerest gratitude to my family and friends for supporting, and patiently tolerating me in my endeavors.

My Valenza Publishing family most definitely deserves praise and admiration for all of their hard work in helping my stories get out to the world, while also allowing me to be undeniably myself. Andrew has always believed in me more than I ever did myself. Dr. Hull, a kindred soul, keeps me on point. Mr. Gunther gets my aesthetic and makes my covers look badass. I appreciate the camaraderie, the sacrifices you all make, and the profound intelligence and creativity you dole out regularly.

I would also like to thank Chris and Jade for their reviews of Thrall, your support and honest reviews helped the story gain traction.

I am ever so grateful for those of you who enjoy reading my stories, rest assured that you are in for a wild ride.

About the Author

J.T. McGee is a former teacher in Saratoga Springs, New York. He is an artist, adventurer, writer and crafter. He takes great pride in the impact that he has had on his students over the years. Since JT was born in the wrong era and can't charge headlong into battle, instead he writes books  and recreates ancient weaponry.

@mrbigbad76 on Instagram and Facebook.

Thank you for reading!

Please consider leaving a review for "Enthralled" on Goodreads!

Valenza Publishing
www.valenzapublishing.com
@valenzapublishing - Instagram/Facebook/Threads
@valenza_publishing - TikTok

And support indie authors by checking out these incredible books!

"Goodwill's Secrets" by Christopher Mele

"Fate's Tether" by Jade Nioma

"A Voice of Life" by Lindsey Forkel

"Witness to the Revolution" by Kiersten Marcil